My Europe

First published as a paperback edition by Patrician Press 2018

E-book edition published by Patrician Press 2018

Copyright for My Europe – A Patrician Press Anthology © Patrician Press 2018

Copyright for each text contributed remains with the author

British Library Cataloguing in Publication Data. A catalogue record for this book is available from the British Library.

ISBN paperback edition 978-1-9997030-0-4

ISBN e-book edition 978-1-9997030-1-1

My Europe

AN ANTHOLOGY

Patrician Press ● Manningtree

Published by Patrician Press 2018
For more information: www.patricianpress.com

Contents

'But if the vote is out, then out goes that impression of what kind of country we are. Around the world we will be seen as the island that cut itself off as a result of anti-foreigner feeling: that will identify us globally more than any other attribute. Our image, our reality, will change overnight.' Polly Toynbee

'In truth, Brussels is a democracy-free zone. From the EU's inception in 1950, Brussels became the seat of a bureaucracy administering a heavy industry cartel, vested with unprecedented law-making capacities. Even though the EU has evolved a great deal since, and acquired many of the trappings of a confederacy, it remains in the nature of the beast to treat the will of electorates as a nuisance that must be, somehow, negated. The whole point of the EU's inter-governmental organisation was to ensure that only by a rare historical accident would democratic mandates converge and, when they did, never restrain the exercise of power in Brussels.' Yanis Varoufakis

'My analysis is that this is a national crisis. There is an aspect of national humiliation associated with what is going on. The triggering of article 50 was so monstrously premature. We're sitting on a grenade with the pin pulled out. I don't see any rainbow at the end of this. The truth is that the EU is a civilising force in international life. Jacques Delors's great achievement was to make sure that the only kind of Europe was a social Europe... What Brexit means is creating divergence from European standards. That process can only be hard, and it will be most painful for many of the people I used to represent.' David Miliband

Anna Johnson

Introduction

When I wrote about hard-edged and dangerous words in the introduction to *Refugees and Peacekeepers,* I was hoping for an end to the dominant narrative of intolerance. Now, in Brexit Britain, I feel astonished at what has slipped our collective memory – the small boy lying still on a Turkish beach, the poppies we wear on Armistice Day. We have forgotten to remember that child and the millions of soldiers and civilians who died for freedom from boundaries and an end to wars caused by nationalism and intolerance. We have given credence to narratives that confirm our own prejudices or suspicions – we have allowed them to divide us. I am worried for my children's future; they have grown up as Europeans. What doors will now be slammed in their faces because of another generation's spite? What conflicts might they have to endure?

It seems to me that we need Promethean patience to make sense of the world, to work out which narratives are reliable; like walking on sand, every step slips a little bit backwards, every truth seems to shift and blur. The mainstream media are in an existentialist 'tale' spin: 'fake' news is just a speedier, digitised version of misinformation and propaganda. Conspiracy theories, once whispered, have become a cacophony. From left wing outlets to the 'alt-right', from libertarian to hard Brexit, the voices that shout loudest are those that echo longest.

In the aftermath of the EU vote, we are living in an uncomfortable limbo: the 'worst of times' and the 'best of times,' misery and rejoicing in equal measure. When opinion is polarised to such an extent, we question who we are – we feel unstable, afraid, angry and desperate. In our Brave New Post-Truth world, judges are Enemies of the People, experts know nothing, our very democracy is under threat.

This instability is felt from root to crown – our government's turmoil reflects that of society: the country is in danger of sleepwalking off a cliff whilst ministers play political games which have everything to do with power, and nothing to do with the good of the nation. We're told that this is the Will of the People, as if it's sacred and inviolable, as if the people can't change their minds – or even object – especially now that it is clear that they voted with inaccurate information. Knowledge of the consequences, of course, was dismissed at the time as gloom and scare-mongering.

I'm sure I'm not the only one who yearns for clarity – a response to the situation we find ourselves in that isn't characterised by hysteria, lies or distortion.

But the truth is out there, and this anthology is one attempt to get the story straight, to explore the idea and the reality of Europe and our place in it, through a variety of sources – expert scrutiny, fiction, poetry, drama and personal testimony.

Our collection opens with a piece by Suzy Adderley, who provides a refreshingly dispassionate summary of the reality and drawbacks of the EU, the reasons why both the political Left and Right can only give it qualified support, and why she herself remains faithful to the European project, despite its grey areas.

Sell your past and buy yourself a future! by Maurizio Ascari is an engaging allegory for our current national confusion. 'Mr Britten's' dynamic plan for self-determination is conceived in optimism and excitement, 'Just think of all the money you're going to save by selling,' he is told. 'Leaving is the right choice! The world is large.' But he has failed to grasp the basic premise of the deal, triggering a 'process that cannot be stopped,' and losing control of what he values the most.

Seven poets have taken up the challenge of distilling the question of Europe into verse. The first, *Take Back Control*, by Attila the Stockbroker pulses with rage and explores the issue of misplaced blame: 'It wasn't the EU who shut your pit down/and sent Met thugs rampaging through your street.' He addresses the central irony of the referendum – that the vote for more control has left us with less – and urges, 'Please don't let UKIP take you for a fool.'

Nostalgia has been in the air recently, particularly a harking back to the time of the empire, when Britain could still claim to be 'great'. Set in a museum with 'Living History' guides, Wersha Bharadwa's witty scenes juxtapose our colonial record of exploitation with contemporary attitudes and prejudices. With perfect irony her parting shot illustrates just how invidious the propaganda about immigration has been.

The Festival of Janus by Mark Brayley, is a poem-parable about duality and division. We are encouraged to take the long view – that it is in our past we may see our present. The mythic horror of its central image serves as a warning to be wary of the 'great orators/the sleek tongued and the forked,' who have used democracy to rouse xenophobia. Hope is reduced to a 'handmade effigy' and the child who carries it can only watch 'how this is played. We are united/only by love/or the blade.'

There are a number of expert writers included in this anthology and it is daily more apparent that – our government being clueless – we need their knowledge. Not gloom and fear but clear-eyed common sense.

James Coiley provides a personal and professional analysis of the implications of Brexit for financial services. We live in a 'transactional age' and London's pre-eminence as the financial capital of Europe is founded on rules, trust and the passport to business. If these are compromised by Brexit then over 10% of national economic output is also put at risk and our multinational capital could become a dull, monochrome and small-minded place.

Catherine Coldstream's *The Conjuring* is a nostalgic piece about our freedom to travel, 'The bus we took was/Magic'. The fingering of coins 'cold as pebbles' in pockets recasts the act of waiting as a kind of meditation 'along the threadbare hours'. This is a poem rich with sensation: 'Mornings were full fat/Camembert'; it celebrates the journey and the experience of being elsewhere but, 'Now less alien,' and enjoying, 'a slice of someone else's time.' How long – one wonders – will this travel-magic endure?

In three languages, *DNA* by Christine De Luca asks how we – as a people – arrived on our island, 'tracking a faint smell of green,' how we 'split from our people' to manage a 'tough land.' We are 'solitary, ambivalent begetters,' a curmudgeonly lot, but it is in our DNA to explore; we are 'related to the whole world' and would do well to remember it.

Uwe Derksen's riposte to Yannis Varoufakis (quoted in the foreword) focuses on British identity, which, he argues, was forged in its imperial past and has never fully resolved itself within a wider European identity. We still find it difficult to integrate and will always harbour a Them and Us mentality.

Michael Dougan is an EU law expert who described the Leave campaign as being guilty of 'dishonesty on an industrial scale' in a lecture just days before the June referendum. A year on he reflects on his predictions and suggests that those who want to see the UK leave the EU are now facing the, 'accountability of reality'. Dougan's analysis shows that the Leave victory was pyrrhic and comes at great cost to the country.

Canon Giles Fraser's opposition to the EU originates in his admiration of the Diggers and the Levellers, early Eurosceptics who fought to, 'lift up that Norman yoke,' and free the 'groaning' English from power exercised from a distance.

Democracy was their antidote and Fraser believes – as they did – that this must lie with the British people, not with unelected bodies of 'covetous, proud men,' who serve profit.

Rick Garboil apparently *Won't Miss EU* as he romps through a pithy review of its highlights including, 'France, with your smelly cheese/or Cyprus with your myrtle trees.' It's jokey but suddenly moving when the punchline arrives: 'Strangers, foreigners, no, you bet/just lots of friends I've not yet met.'

Cecilia Hall's *European Family* has its origins across the continent. They are cosmopolitan, adventurous and creative people who lived fascinating lives against a backdrop of turbulent world events. Among these affectionate recollections there is also pain and regret: the writer talks about the rejection of herself, her mother and sister by her British grandparents after the war as an open wound in the family, aggravated by the xenophobia of the referendum. She would have us remember that unity is strength and our divisions superficial.

We Europeans by Andrea Inglese is poetic working-out of the nature of European identity – is it a territory, a mindset, a history? Warlords, artists, philosophers, even Hitler, can all be described as European. In the end there is ambiguity: this disloyal, dangerous, avant-garde group is defined by being indefinable.

We're on firmer ground with Helena Kennedy QC, who reminds us that law matters in the Brexit negotiations. We have legal obligations in Europe and trying to cut and run without paying our dues is both unlawful and unethical. More worrying still is that laws and law givers are under attack. They are not our enemy, Kennedy assures us, but our protectors and we must protect them, or walk away from safety and security: 'The price of its loss will be very high indeed.'

Jean McHale points out the practicalities of imposing the too-simple answers of Brexit on another complex system – health care. If reciprocal health care ends, for example, Brits can look forward to paying for treatment abroad upfront. The NHS is already chronically understaffed; losing the 5% of workers who come from other EU member states would be disastrous. EU directives are often dismissed as 'red tape', but when they safeguard the quality and safety of blood and organs, it is dangerous to treat them so lightly – the 'health of the nation' is at stake.

Petra McQueen's *Fall Out* is the second of the collection's two short stories. Sophie and Jake's marriage is on the line the day after the referendum – he's a 'fascist', she's a 'libtard loser'. Their rift mirrors that in British society – their conflict is ours.

The taking of sides over Europe has been painful, it has a human cost. This tale is funny and sad – the murder of Jo Cox, MP was tragic.

Why does Giacinto Palmieri up sticks from Milan to begin a new life and job in London? *Because I can*, he tell us, and he revels in his adopted country. Native customs like the office Christmas party unleash his creativity and he finds himself doing stand-up comedy and supporting West Ham. His hope is that Brexit doesn't stop people like him from offering skills, comedy and football supporting zeal – the country will be a poorer place without immigrants who appreciate it and enrich it in ways that we cannot imagine.

Future in the Cards is the inspiration for Robert Ronsson's allegorical short story. He focuses on tribal boys and the etiquette of football card trading or 'swapsies'. In this grubby but innocent playtime society, the gang is all; our hero decides to leave its protection and go it alone. But free trade doesn't come with bargain-

ing power and a 'four for one' swap is a desperate price to pay –
for a small boy and a small country.

The clear-eyed economy of Lemn Sissay's personification of
Brexit makes it compelling. We all recognise the aftermath of relationship break-ups – the recrimination, the reassessment, the real-
isation that it was for the best, 'He was a bully…a control freak'.
But what of the Leaver? He has doubts too, things he misses
that 'he didn't notice at the time.' In the end, nobody wants to
dance with this particular, impoverished 'island' and that might be
poignant if it didn't give rise to dangerous things like hate, the taking of sides and plotting for a fight.

Ken Smith tells us about finding his *Inner European* through
tracing his German mother's family. This is a physical as well as
an emotional journey, as the author travels to his mother's beloved
'Heimat,' where he receives a warm and open hearted welcome.
The process of fitting pieces of his identity back together and, 'all
this remembering,' sharpens the author's 'hunger for harmony.' He
would like to see more, 'gratitude – for the decades of peace since
1945.'

George Szirtes' choice of title *Je suis Européen* is a declaration
– a 'badge'. But when he talks about 'a vast silence,' behind that
badge, there is a sense that the voices that 'speak the city into
ordered being' are no longer being heard, or listened to. In fact we
are in danger of forgetting our history, our dead, 'everything we
have made and have deserved.' Those 'statues with open mouths,'
are there to remind us of the 'reasons for living here,' they embody
ideas about freedom and hope that perhaps the 'background
musak/we all move to' has drowned out.

Stephen Timms is a longstanding MP, beloved of his constituents. His defence of the EU is rooted in his care for the people
he has represented for 23 years. His discussion ranges from his
local Tate and Lyle sugar refinery, to Rolls Royce in Derby, Nissan

in Sunderland and finally, UK financial services. He explains why leaving the single market and the customs union will cause an 'economic dislocation blighting the lives of tens of thousands.' The government will 'never be forgiven' for letting the public down so badly. His fight to avert disaster continues.

The final piece in our anthology is *Inside the Bubble* by Heather Welford. A chance encounter on a train exposes the cheerful thoughtlessness of a Brexit supporter. The author captures the shock of encountering not just an opposing view but an unreasoning one – born of prejudice. There is sadness here and frustration that the simple explanations are so easy to latch onto, so hard to dislodge and so rooted in xenophobia and nationalism. To leave Europe is to retreat into ourselves when we need to see the bigger picture, the 'planet-sized' problems we should be solving together.

This collection is about challenging dominant narratives and remembering what we value and hold dear. Vote Leave's narrative was simple and easy to remember, as lies often are – sadly the truth wasn't loud or catchy enough. I hope that these writings go some way to explaining why it is crucial that we continue to scrutinise the information we are given, to question and object. The writers in this anthology talk about being 'taken in' by false promises, they explore scapegoating, division, the importance of peace, history, law, health, trade, identity, and freedom of movement. Relationships are key here. Our relationship with Europe may not be perfect, but it has made us prosperous, culturally rich, and peaceful. Now there are many people who feel desperately sad and dejected at the prospect of becoming isolated. There are many other people who expected the British lion to go romping across the global savannah sweeping all before it. Who's going to come clean?

Time is running out for our weak government – it's deal or die – parliament and the people need the whole story this time. This fundamental issue should not be decided by tribal politics, short term power-play or lies on the side of buses – our children's future is at stake. Our small island will diminish and fade if it turns its back on its friends, its closest trading partners, its connection to the world. I don't remember seeing 'Poorer, weaker, meaner,' on the side of any buses. Can this really be the plan?

Brexit – Neither Black Nor White

Suzy Adderley

The mainstream news media are continually attempting to make Brexit a party issue and to force politicians into an unequivocal position on leaving the EU, but the situation is more complicated than that; and there are ideological reasons why both the main parties are split, and reasons that are concerned with the nature of the EU itself.

The EU, whilst representing a consensus of alliance intended to prevent further wars is primarily a trading partnership in the neoliberal tradition. The principles of free trade have been bound to policies of free movement of labour and a common regulatory environment. Many decisions within the agreements are made, however, by unelected bodies which are fundamentally undemocratic and secretive, working primarily in the interests of corporations. The punishment by austerity of countries within Europe who get into debt through the imbalances brought about by being tied into the single currency is exacerbating inequality among the member states.

For many Tories, the neoliberal stance of the EU is not problematic, but free movement of labour and the loss of sovereignty are anathema, while for left-wing Socialists, the neoliberal structures are highly problematic whilst they would support the free movement of labour and regulatory structures. So it seems to me unreasonable to expect either main party, as presently constituted, to as a whole or entirely support or reject Brexit.

The referendum, originally promised by David Cameron in 2013 to head off the threats from UKIP and his Eurosceptic MPs, now leaves both parties still split and desiring to cherry pick the aspects of the EU to which they are sympathetic. The United Kingdom as a country finds itself in increasing conflict and in danger of breaking apart through the ramifications of the minority decision.

I find myself still a Remainer because of the financial and regulatory consequences of leaving, because I support the 'four freedoms' of freedom of movement of goods, capital, labour and services and because I think we should be attempting to reform the EU from within rather than without. Since I voted to Remain in the European Economic Community in 1975, I have come to feel myself a European and have welcomed this expansion of identity. I may be against the neoliberal nature of the EU and some of its undemocratic structures but I have never changed my mind about the advantages of membership.

If I were a member of the government at this critical time, I would organise a series of public debates that would include a broad spectrum of financial, environmental and other experts and then conduct a detailed public opinion survey that contained questions on all the major and minor issues. Based on this, the government would decide whether to continue the Brexit negotiations or request a dismissal of Article 50. This would require only an admission that the campaign leading up to the referendum had been too simplistic, that voters had not been in possession of enough information at the time of the vote and that any achievable withdrawal might neither meet the expectations of the Leavers or avoid severe consequences to the UK, to Northern Ireland and to the many EU and UK citizens living abroad.

Sell Your Past and Buy Yourself a Future!

Maurizio Ascari

I had been thinking of selling my house for a while. Since I retired I had cherished the idea of relocating and starting a new life. Far from the northern city where I had slaved my existence away. Far from the long hours of commuting. Far from greasy tables and lonely dinners. Far from it all.

Where should I go? A small town in Devon? Or perhaps Cornwall? Or should I opt for the sunnier beaches and milder winters of southern Spain? And what about Sicily? I had not made up my mind yet, but the idea of selling appealed to me precisely because it marked a new beginning. Selling was a promise of happiness, a way to cancel, at a single stroke, the monotony of an endless routine, the greyness of middle age, all that made my life heavy and dull and simply not worth living.

This is how it all began. There was a new estate agent in the high street close to the road where I lived, called *BestSellers & Co.* The guy who welcomed me with a big smile, was outgoing and smart. Perfectly dressed in a grey suit, pink shirt and a rainbow-hued tie that was hard to miss.

The place was spotlessly tidy. Big posters of smiling people shaking hands. A slogan – Sell Your Past and Buy Yourself a Future! – was printed in red letters on a mirror that covered the wall behind the desk. I could not help seeing those words as meant for me.

'I'm bent on selling. It's not a big house, but sunny, good spaces. Two bedrooms.'

'You did well to come to us,' was the reply. 'We have plenty of clients who are looking for a house exactly like yours. Of course, we can also help you choose a new one, if you are interested. There is a wide range on offer,' he said, pointing to the slimmest and largest of computer screens.

I was asked to sign a form. To clarify that I was entrusting them with the exclusive sale and no other agent would be given authority to sell at the same time. That was fine by me. I was not in a hurry to get rid of my house, although I felt this urge to change my life. Moving would be a new beginning, an upgrade. The word 'romance' flashed like a neon light in my mind. Everything would be possible.

The following day they came to see the house. I mean, Nigel – the nice guy I had been talking to – and an associate called Boris. Blond hair. Very much the artist type. Great fun. Together they toured the place. A whirlwind of jokes and witty remarks.

'Just think of all the money you're going to save by selling,' said Nigel, while Boris nodded approvingly.

'It's calculated that a two-bedroom house like yours costs 350 quid a month in terms of sheer maintenance,' continued Nigel, 'excluding all the rest – insurance, taxes, bills, whatever. Running a house is ruinous these days.'

'You do well to sell, Mr Britten. Leaving is the right choice! The world is large. Buy yourself a place in a warm climate. Do away with heating bills. I envy you. I do. Unfortunately I have to remain because of my business. Otherwise I would follow in your foot-steps. To leave or not to leave, that is the question,' he quipped with a laugh.

'One vote in favour of Mr Britten's leaving,' added Nigel, genially displaying his crown of very white teeth. 'Another vote!' echoed Boris, raising his right hand to the ceiling, his left hand promptly following, as if he found it hard to resist Nigel's enthusiasm.

After a brief consultation, the two came up with a price of £199,999.

'A small signature to confirm that you agree on the price, and the formalities are over,' said Nigel while handing me a form.

'A nice pile of money, Mr Britten,' said Boris. 'Especially if you move to an area where life is cheaper.'

'Property is just a burden, I'm afraid,' sympathised Nigel.

'A burden,' chimed in his colleague.

'So I'll have to start looking for a new place, after all,' I replied, feeling both excited and tired, 'but there is time. Houses often take a long time to sell.'

'You are in the hands of *BestSellers*... Nothing to worry about.'

They asked me for the keys, so that they might show the place to potential customers. Their schedule was busy and this was the usual procedure.

After seeing them to the door, where Boris cracked a parting joke ('The die is cast, as Caesar said after ordering his salad! Ha ha!'), I came back to the sitting room. The smell of Nigel's cigar was still in the air. I did not know why, but I suddenly felt that the future looked hazy.

The first purchaser materialised ten days later. It was actually a couple. Very young. Cash buyers. I wondered how they had managed to put together so much cash in the space of such a short life... rich parents? Winning the lottery? Money laundering? They looked at room after room with expressionless faces. No glance exchanged. No goodbye said. Nice people.

Other visitors followed, more than I actually met, since a couple of times I found one of the sticky notes that I kept on the hall table with something scribbled on it. Just Hello there! Or Many thanks! Or Buyers impressed!

One Monday morning, I was confronted by a new member of the Nigel gang.

Bell ringing. Door opening. 'My name is Nicola,' said a young lady, extending her right hand, while an old lady with thick lenses was leaning on her left arm. Nicola had a slight Scottish accent. Nice figure. Engaging ways. I immediately took to her, for she was sweet, and yet she was definitely an independent woman.

After showing the house to the old lady, who found it difficult to climb the stairs and concluded a flat would be more suitable, Nicola turned to me, suddenly conspiratorial.

'Between ourselves, Mr Britten, I intend to set up an estate agency of my own. Working for *BestSellers* has been an interesting experience, but it's over. There's not much they can teach me there. Need to be on me own.' She positively winked at me and I'm afraid I actually reddened.

'This is my private number. Should you need any help in the future, buying or selling, contact me directly.'

I could not help smiling at her sense of initiative. Somebody who would leave no stone unturned – not even the stone of Scone! – to reach her goal. A born leader.

'I'll have my own business by then,' she went on in a matter of fact tone, as if she had read this in her crystal ball. 'I already have a name for it: Selling No Problem. SNP for those who are in the know. It's an acronym, you know. People love cyphers.' Another wink. 'Cheerio.'

Two months later I received a phone call. It was a woman's voice. 'Is that Mr Britten speaking?'

'Yes, it's me.'

'I'm calling from *BestSellers*. My name is Theresa.' Her confident voice was not devoid of sex-appeal. I pictured a brunette. 'We're proud to tell you that your house has been sold.'

I was taken aback. I was flabbergasted. I was...

After a second, I regained control.

'Wait a minute. You're telling me that you've found a buyer, a potential buyer, which I am happy to hear, but I've not decided yet. There's plenty of things to consider.'

'Well, actually, I'm telling you that your house has been *sold*. I meant precisely what I said.'

'Is this a bad joke? May I talk to your colleague, Nigel? He's such a nice person. I'm sure there must be a misunderstanding. Perhaps you're thinking of a different house.'

'Well, Nigel no longer works here.'

'What do you mean?'

'He's reached the target he had set for himself. Selling 400 houses in 400 days. He's now moved on to something else. He said he needs new challenges.'

'How can he have sold 400 houses in 400 days? Come on... That's hard to believe!'

'I can assure you.'

'Anyway, he's not sold MY house! There's plenty of papers to be signed to sell a house, and I will sell only if I want to.'

'I regret to inform you that you've already made your decision.'

'What?'

'There's your signature on this form, which clearly states that you give us authority to sell your house to any buyer at any time at a price to be agreed. You agreed on the price, so there's no backing away from this.'

'Wait a minute! I've never heard of anything like that. I'm sure it's illegal. It's absurd! Ridiculous!'

'You've made your intentions clear. You triggered a process that cannot be stopped. It's you who have chosen this. It's you who wanted to sell. If you'll excuse me, I've got other calls to make.' The voice was now distant, impersonal. 'Whenever possible, come to see us or contact us. We need the details of your bank account. As agreed, we'll deduct our percentage and deposit the rest. I wish you a good day, Mr Britten.'

Click.

I sat in silence, staring out of the bedroom window, my mobile still in my hand, my head not even turning, just immobile, as if this was a dream.

'Are they all crazy?' I found myself uttering.

I looked at my house, all around me, which was no longer mine. My bed, my desk, my walls. My slippers under the bedside table. Every single item was just part of a whole. I had taken all this for granted, but now...

What about the new life I wanted to start? Was I simply losing my old one? I had not asked for this. You need to see clearly before taking a definitive step.

Actually, I still liked my house. I would go to the agency and demand to talk to Nigel. It was he, after all, who had made me sign the form. I threw myself face down on the quilt and fell asleep, my head strangely pulsing.

'This contract is legally binding. There's nothing you can do about it. I'm sorry.' Such was the opinion of the solicitors' firm I consulted – *Supreme & Court* – the highest experts in this field, as I had been assured by a neighbour who had taken interest in my case, or pity on me.

'You should have read what you signed more carefully,' was their verdict.

'But you know how it is these days. Any time you visit a bank or any office they just ask you to sign plenty of paper. All you can do is trust them.'

'Well, you're a grown-up man, Mr. Britten.'

I dejectedly left the neo-Gothic building where *Supreme & Court* had their premises. No shred of hope remained.

I had two months to get out of my house. Only, I did not want to. Oh, Trenton-upon-Tyne was not the best place to live perhaps, but I had grown used to it.

A sudden impulse led me out into the open air, with no direction in mind. In about an hour I found myself at Heddon, where Hadrian's Wall still rose. I walked along the wall, which spoke to my imagination. A line crossing the land, cutting it in two. Before and after. Here and there.

I found myself standing on what remained of the wall, like a child, suddenly happy.

The Romans and the Picts. The wall was meant to keep others away, but it could be crossed so easily these days. I thought of the many tourists who came to visit the spot from all over the world. I liked mixing with this assortment of people. Being in a crowd made me feel less lonely. No space was left for sadness.

While I was walking home along a street that was bustling with life in the late afternoon, I thought I saw Nigel sitting at a café on the opposite side of a busy street. Buses and cars were speeding both ways. I ran to the nearest zebra crossing. When I reached the café he was no longer there. Perhaps he had never been...

What about the owners of the other 399 houses he had recently sold? I might still reach them. We might at least work it through together. But then, they were probably happier than me.

And if I took a plane and rushed off to Sicily or the Costa del Sol? Sea and sun. An endless summer. I was no longer young. I looked at my face in a shop window. Not a single hair standing on my head. Gold-rimmed glasses. I felt so vulnerable, old age gaining on me.

I just want to stay here. This is my place. This is the town where I grew up, where my friends – ok, maybe acquaintances – live, where the baker says Hello in the morning and where I can have a pint of beer at the same pub I frequented with my workmates when I left the office. This is my place!

A day went by. Two days. A week went by without my doing anything about relocating to a distant place. My plan had lost its meaning. Only now did I realise that I was still attached to my old life. Sicily would be good for a holiday.

I put all my things in a container. The empty house looked like a shell that had once contained my life. I could not imagine another container. Or rather, I *could* have. I had certainly entertained the idea, but not this way. Not this way.

I drove to Newcastle and spent the first night sitting in the station, pretending to wait for my train. A white haired bearded guy addressed me in a friendly tone, 'Are you a homeless yourself?'

Honestly, he looked as if he had not taken a good bath in ages, but he inspired trust in me. 'Actually I am,' I found myself admitting. It was technically true.

'There's not enough social housing in this country,' was his reply. 'I'm just Jeremy, who spends his nights sleeping in a cardboard box, but if I was a politician things would change. Only, people like us never get to sit in those big Houses in London. We just sit here... Sit and wait.'

'If you were a politician I'd probably vote for you,' I said, not knowing why. Was I just being kind?

In the morning I drove back and took a room. I showered and shaved and walked out to a café.

I was walking slowly, face downward, when I happened to lift my eyes. Nigel was beaming at me from the other side of a glass pane. Above him a big bold slogan: Rent Your Happiness, Now!

'I can't believe it,' were the words that formed on my lips. I felt my fist clenching, my blood rising.

'Mr Britten!' The guy was on the threshold of the shop, offering his hand to me, a full-blown smile on his smooth face. 'I never forget a name. It's my job. Is there anything I can do for you?'

I let myself be led into the shop, where a gallery of cosy interiors was on display.

'Do you wish to rent a place, Mr Britten? I've moved to a new branch. It seems many people wish to get rid of all the nuisances and risks property-owning entails. Renting is so simple. Just the best way to live. Letting other people take care of it all.'

My eyes fell on a nice little sitting room. It looked so beautifully familiar. 'But that... That's my window!'

'Your window? I doubt it, Mr Britten, but it can become so. What wonderful insight you have! What a keen eye! Yes, this is precisely the house you sold. I still remember the couple who came to see it, also because they popped in just a couple of days ago. They've realised they don't *really* need the house. So they are renting it. Is there any chance you might be interested? The price's dirt cheap.'

After signing a contract, which I read over and over again, I obtained the keys to my house. I was suddenly happy. It took me less than a week to bring all my furniture back and to be comfortably installed in my own house.

A few weeks later I met Nigel once again. As elegant as ever. Life whirling like a merry-go-round around him. 'Mr Britten. What a nice surprise! Good to see you walking so straight. You look much better than the last time I saw you.' His happily mobile face made you feel that this was the best of all possible worlds.

'There's something I've been wanting to tell you for a while,' he added. 'I've been thinking of your smart move. What a clever sod you are! Let me congratulate you. Back in your house and when there's a problem it's somebody else who deals with it. The good life, Mr. Britten. You've opted for the good life.'

I did not have time to reply, for his mobile rang and he was already walking away, deeply engaged in conversation with a customer. I turned and saw his back against the setting sun. *What an energetic person*, I could not help thinking, despite everything. *We really need people like him to keep the world on the move.* Then I headed home.

Take Back Control

Attila the Stockbroker

You tell me how you've suffered since the closure.
I see the pain and sadness in your eyes.
I feel your anger at our country's leaders
Who offer only platitudes and lies.
At gigs I hear so many of these stories.
All different, but the message is the same.
You're sick to death of scheming politicians.
No longer going to play their poxy game.

The referendum was your chance. You took it.
They told you we'd be taking back control.
Control of jobs and factories and borders:
A revolution wrapped up in a poll.
The EU is a ghastly corporate bully.
Cheap labour and big profits at its core.
I understand why you voted for Brexit:
One chance to strike a blow in the class war.

But it wasn't the EU who shut your pit down
And sent Met thugs rampaging through your street.
They didn't close your hospitals and workshops,
Smash down your union to brave defeat.
No EU diktat caused the housing crisis,
The poll tax, bedroom tax or zero hours.
No, all of these were brought in by the Tories —
And soon those bastards will have brand new powers.

So let's take back control with strong trade unions
And let's take back control and organise.
Take back control of pub and school and workplace
And counter all the endless media lies.
Take back control as we all stand together.
No scapegoating and no divide and rule.
The future is unwritten, and it's daunting.
Please don't let UKIP take you for a fool.

Living History

Wersha Bharadwa

The casting notice said: 'British Asian actors needed to play specific individuals from history.' The museum had won some sort of heritage funding to acknowledge the contributions South Asians and those from the subcontinent had made to the expansion of Western Europe. I jumped at the chance. The last paid gig I'd had was dressing up as Elsa at a kid's *Frozen* party. And I audition, but am just not peachy-skinned enough for most of the BBC, ITV and Netflix period dramas. 'Wonderful, Reena. We'll be in touch'. I'm used to it. With more of these alternative 'living history' diversity type projects, you hope someone in TV pays attention and I play an Asian hero in a costume drama soon. Anyway. I thought I'd share with you the following collected and abbreviated transcripts from my time working as a 'living exhibit' at the museum. There was an intense training process, which meant extensive reading up on the women I was asked to portray and also on the era. It was extreme method acting: I had to live and breathe the characters. And because students and museum visitors, AKA 'The Public', will ask lots of questions, (regularly bordering on the insane as you'll read below) sticking purely to the facts gets challenging and awkward. So you drink your way through lunch with the other actors to drown your creative sorrows...

Starring: Me as Jind Kaur

Teacher: Ok, class. Here we are at the Living History Museum. The actors are dressed as famous characters from European and British history and you can ask them any question you want. How exciting!

Me: Come in, come in. I am Jind Kaur. It's a pleasure to meet you all. I am the first documented Sikh woman in Britain and the Maharani of Punjab in India. I've spent most of my life fighting the British Empire. The consequences of losing the Sikh wars against them have been dire. My son, Duleep Singh, was torn away from me and taken into British custody when he was just nine years old. I kept on fighting to have him returned to me. Duleep and I were finally reunited last year and I've been here, in England, ever since.

Teacher: Now remember everyone, you're getting graded on this. So think about your questions before asking.

Student #1: What year is it now?

Me: 1862. My health is bad but good things are finally happening. I'm teaching my son about the atrocities of British rule. The taxes on farmers. The starving villagers. Duleep has been brainwashed at Queen Victoria's court. They've converted him to Christianity, taught him Shakespeare – he has forgotten everything about his culture. I might look frail and old, but trust me, I'm preparing for him to take India back! Duleep is a Punjabi king. Not the lapdog of imperialist oppressors.

Student #1: I read Duleep Singh was really close to Queen Victoria. Like... she actually loved him.

Me: How wonderful for you to be reading about their relationship. But can you see where there might be a problem with that? It's exactly why I've been asked to meet you; to help reflect the rich and diverse voices and points of view in history.

Student #1: So you don't think it was true?

Me: It would be a strange love wouldn't it? The Queen and her government have taken over my homeland by force, along with my son. She is now called the Empress of India.

Student #2: If Indians were so clever, why did you allow yourselves to be colonised? Doesn't that just prove the British were inherently more powerful?

Me: I never thought of it that way. But, yes, you could be right. Being quick to subjugate other people is quite the accomplishment.

Student #3: I just wanna say how cool you are. Fighting as a woman and stuff.

Me: Thank you.

Student #4: Do you have WIFI here?

Me: What?

Student #3: They should make a film about you. You rock.

Me: They are.

Teacher: Hang on, are we in the present day or past?

Me: Present. But only for 10 seconds—

Student #3: Awesome! Who's playing Jind Kaur?

Me: Taylor Swift.

Starring: Me, as Cornelia Surabji

Me: Please enter. I am Cornelia Surabji. I am the first woman to sit the civil law exams in the UK at Somerville College in Oxford in 1893. I am also India's first female barrister.

Visitor #1: Surely another woman would've come before you?

Me: You'd think wouldn't you? But, no. However, I was denied the government of India scholarship for my studies in England – as a woman, you see. But I have the most wonderful friends here, the Hobhouse family. They've sponsored my education and are very dear to my heart.

Visitor #2: What's an average day like for you?

Me: Was there ever such a thing! I mainly write and campaign for secluded Indian women. They're called 'purdahnashins'. Let me see... I'm writing a book. Oh, and – finally – I've become a member of Lincoln's Inn.

Visitor #2: What's that?

Me: My goodness, sir! Why, it's where barristers like myself are called to the Bar.

Starring: Me, as Princess Sophia Duleep Singh

Me: Hello everyone. My name is Sophia Duleep Singh. I'm a princess, a suffragette and a member of the Women's Social and Political Union who are helping women to win the right to vote.

Visitor #1: Is this one of those PC things? Because there weren't any immigrants in in those days. This is historically inaccurate.

Me: How? I am alive and well in London.

Visitor #2: Where's the dinosaurs section?

Me: –

Visitor #1: I watch Downton Abbey and stuff. There are no Asian or Black people in those shows. They – sorry, you – weren't around.

Me: Mmm hmm.

Starring: Me, as a 15th-century lascar's daughter

Me: Hi everyone. Welcome aboard our ship. My father came to Europe via Vasco Da Gama's maritime route. My name's Emma. My father converted from Islam to Christianity and married my mother.

A college student: Is it nice working on a cruise liner? I'm thinking of career options.

Me: Good for you! Many of my father's friends jumped ship because of maltreatment and 18-hour days. They'd been forced to work for a pittance. But I'm sure it won't be the case for you.

A college student: You haven't heard of any graduate schemes.

Me: Graduate schemes? Well... No.

Starring: Me, as a widow of an Indian soldier who fought at Dunkirk

Me: Welcome. Welcome. I'm Ayesha Khan. I'm the wife of an Indian soldier who fought at Dunkirk. Great to see you all so interested in this forgotten history. I'm the first –

Student #1: Miss? There's an actual soldier in the next room – can we see him?

Teacher: After this, yes.

Me: I won't take up too much of your time.

Student #1: He has a gun and everything!

Starring: Me as a shop owner in the 1800s

Me: Hi everyone. I'm Sita Devi–

Visitor #1: Is this like the olden day version of an Asian shop?

Me: What's an Asian shop? I'm a Victorian pharmacist.

Visitor #2: Yeah, but don't you sell a little bit of everything, even though it's a chemist?

Me. Uh...well yes... I do have sweets and some hardware essentials alongside medicines. Is that what you're asking?

Finally, the following transcripts are excerpts from conversations and questions I've been asked while playing any one of the characters above on various occasions. I did say we often drank beers at lunch, but some days, when things got really stimulating, I'd slip out of character. Please forgive my unprofessionalism in advance...

Visitor #1: What I can't understand is, if it's so bad here, why don't you go back to your own country?

Me: I was born here. Next?

Visitor #2: I'm really into my heritage too, so I think your work is great.

Me: Thank you.

Visitor #2: I traced back my ancestry and I come from a proud and strong lineage of slave-owners.

Visitor #3: That's inappropriate.

Me: It's ok.

Visitor #3: Well I think his ancestors were giant vibrators.

Visitor #2: What did she say?

Me: He said your ancestors were the greatest.

Visitor: #4: I think if we're being honest, the Empire wasn't *that* bad. You have the railroads in India–

Me: Oh fuckinghellmotherfuckingbullshitting...

Visitor #4: Excuse me?

Me: Sorry, can you repeat the question? I just want to make sure I heard you right.

Visitor #4: The British Empire wasn't bad? Like everyone's still benefiting from it.

Me: I think you'd enjoy visiting room 101. That's where you get to meet with the ghosts of the Jallianwala Bagh Massacre.

Visitor #4: The what?

Me: The massacre. The one where the British Army, led by General Dyer, opened fire on a peaceful crowd of demonstrators which included children and women. But do take a jacket please. You'll find it's pretty frosty in there.

Visitor #5: What it is for me is, I don't like it when foreigners tell us what to do.

Me: Yes. I understand. And I'm sure the Royal Family would agree. Oh wait.

Visitor #6: I understand your feelings towards colonisation. That's why I voted Leave. The whole thing with Europe felt like my country was being colonised, you know?

Me: Hang on a second. You voted to leave the EU because you were scared of being colonised?

The Festival of Janus

Mark Brayley

Rough winds blew in
from the very home of democracy
and circled above the plaza.
Dust, crows and scraps of paper,
unsettled by the zephyr, swirled above.
Below, low-faced crones read oracles of no,
oracles of woe, but never dared to know.
Faces twisted in loss and impotent anger,
wanting nothing more than bread.
Their undirected rage set to sail
and steered to and fro
for the full force gusts of Mediterranean heat,
half a world away.
And at the heart of this throng,
Sinis, reborn and wet with viscera,
awaiting the ghost of Theseus' blade,
bent two pines, again and again,
and tied the people, one by one,
by the ankles,
before releasing them.

Moving through the crowd,
hailing the oracular visions
of bathing in asps' milk,
the great orators,
the sleek tongued and the forked,
wearing paper thin masks
for the festival of Janus,
offered the sky, or the sky
falling in.
They knew full well that
democracy and xenophobia
both have common roots.
Behind their eyes were visions
of false empires, orgies
and a woken beast.

Between their legs crawled a child,
bearing a handmade effigy
of hope,
bound for the temple of Janus.
Mute in all but whispers,
she clung to the figure.

At the centre of it all,
the vast arched gate of the temple of Janus
stood before her, the doors held shut
against what may be.
Around its balconies and columns were deities
in every aspect of the pantheon:
Saturn, turning his back
on his children and the Golden Age;
Minerva, lost in lament for knowledge;

Juno – she who reminds people –
weeping openly;
Jupiter, throwing down thunder and lightning
with total disregard for mere mortals;
Proudest of all, Janus,
with his two faces,
looking at both the moon
and the rising sun,
surrounded by snakes
eating their own tails,
stood as a guardian
of the present.
The infinite present.

Beyond the great arches,
on the other side of the temple,
treaties, as old as Troy,
were torn asunder.
Rising dust from the hooves of his horse,
Cadmus rode out in search of his lost sister.
His kidnapped kin.
Fruitless in his search,
he found distraction
in slaying other dragons
along his way, until his mission
was but a memory. The world
no longer wondered whether
he would have wept
when he wed his Harmonia.
And so it goes.

A silver haired man was preaching
at the foot of the temple,
and the child, at the foot of the silver haired man,
listened to, but only half heard,
his words.
He spoke of the Iani and I-and-I,
and he spoke of an eye for an eye.
Bellyful, he was bellicose
and the child placed
her effigy at his feet
and looked up.

'The gate,' he said,
'The Portae Belli.
Look on it, if you dare,' he said,
pointing to the doors of the temple of Janus.
'The gate will open,
if we do not proceed with care.'
Then he noticed the child and,
bending low,
said, 'Watch now how this is played.
We are united
only by love
or by the blade.'

Why Brexit Matters to Banks and Why Banks Matter to Us

James Coiley

I have an unfashionable emotional attachment to the idea of Europe. Through childhood and early adulthood national borders seemed to fold away like cardboard after Christmas. The contributors to that sense of opening were disparate – the rise of no-frills air travel was probably as important as the lifting of the Iron Curtain – but the direction of travel seemed certain. Now the walls are being remade, to be constructed in equal parts of barbed wire and paper-work. Undoubtedly mine is a privileged perspective, and you don't need to look far to the east and south to understand that there are many for whom the notion of freedom of movement is altogether less abstract. Nevertheless, I feel sadness that the freedom to travel, study and work, as of right, across a continent of 500 million people and many disparate cultures is not more valued. I think we will miss it when it's gone; to get a real sense of homecoming it pays to have been away for a while.

However, we live in a transactional age. So let's put sentiment aside and look at the emerging impact of the UK's decision to

leave the European Union on the shape and size of the UK economy. That may be a little dry for some tastes, but this matters.
The compounding nature of growth means that percentage points
foregone now will not easily be recouped later. The difference will
be felt in myriad interactions with healthcare, with social care,
with education, with benefits and pensions, with the stuff and fab-
ric of the world around us. I will talk primarily about financial
services, because that is what I know best. That also may take
some justification given recent history. Banks (and the rest) – who
needs them? Well, industry body The CityUK thinks that the financial services industry employs 2.2 million across the UK, most of
them outside London[i]. Those people together contribute around
10.7% of the national economic output – this is one of the few sectors where the UK has a trade surplus – and the industry and its
employees together account for 11.5% of the UK's total tax rev-
enue[ii]. You don't have to accept those figures in their entirety,
and there are more than respectable grounds to think that it might
be a good thing if the UK did a little less banking and little more
making. Whatever your particular national priorities, however, it
strikes me that it might be a good thing to pause and reflect before
handing away a good portion of the national income.

From early in the referendum process I was working my way
around the City of London in my professional capacity as a financial services lawyer, engaging with audiences who were in varying
degrees passionate, sceptical, worried, confused or bored. We
looked at the process for exiting, and the political context to that
process. We looked at the available models for future co-existence
with the remainder of the EU. We looked at how markets and
economies might react. Much of our collective speculation was
awry, particularly on immediate market impacts. UK politics has
been a nerve-jangling procession of the unexpected. Many of our
observations, however are emerging as fact with the inevitability

of a calving iceberg; you know that it will fall off sometime soon. Chief among them is that large parts of the UK's financial service industry depend on ready access to consumers of their services in mainland Europe, and that an extended period of uncertainty around that access would result in the export of people and capital across the North Sea, Irish Sea and English Channel.

Cross-border financial services – the shortest possible introduction

To understand why, we need to look at how the finance industry in the EU works across borders. As of today, the 28 countries of the EU represent a single market for financial services, albeit an imperfect one in many respects. An investment bank established in London can market its services to a customer in Portugal on the basis of a regulatory passport. Essentially, the Portuguese regulator acknowledges that it is unnecessary for it to supervise the bank, because its British counterpart is already doing so on the basis of more-or-less the same rulebook. The same is true in reverse, of course, but less so; over time, despite periodic initiatives by its European counterparts, London has become the *de facto* financial capital of an entire continent. With that domestic market on its doorstep, London rivals and in some markets surpasses the scale of New York.

Take away the passport, and the bank needs the customer to come to London. The customer, however, may not want to, because it feels more comfortable transacting in its home jurisdiction. It may not need to, because there are rival local providers. It may not even be allowed to, for good or bad regulatory reasons. The inevitable outcome is that the bank acquires office space and a banking licence in Lisbon, or more likely another financial centre where passporting remains available. There will be a dialogue with the local regulator, where the agenda on the one side is to minimise cost and disruption and on the other to ensure that that the new desks are filled by warm bodies. From there on, the trend is set. If your traders and salesmen are in a given location, then ultimately so also will be your board members, risk managers, book-keepers and (yes, I'm afraid so) lawyers. One of the pleasures of working in the City is the multi-national nature of its work-force but the flipside is that, for better or worse, a large part of that workforce is highly footloose. All else – offices, restaurants, schools, construction workers, chefs and teachers – will follow over time.

There are other visions of how this plays out, some of them with a basis in fact or law. One alternative to a regulatory passport which has been touted is the notion of regulatory equivalence – that is, broadly, the recognition by one regulator that the rule book of another is sufficiently credible such that financial institutions in the jurisdiction of the latter can be permitted access. If the princi-ples sounds similar, the quality is different – equivalence regimes are fragmentary and the grant of equivalence status is a favour which is re-assessed as rules evolve, to be extended or withdrawn on a regulatory whim. Importantly, equivalence decisions have proven to be highly politicised, which may not be a good thing in light of increasingly ill-tempered exit discussions.

Another repackaging of much the same basic product is mutual recognition by way of a free trade agreement in financial services. That deals with many of the issues inherent in relying on equiva-lence and as such would unquestionably be a good outcome for the UK financial sector. Unfortunately, given the rhetoric and motiva-tions of the parties involved, it currently seems an unlikely one.

Some will welcome this. Passporting, equivalence, recognition – all require London and the rest of the EU to march in step to varying degrees. There are certainly elements of EU financial reg-ulation which are ill-designed, possibly ill-suited to the UK financial landscape. Why not seize the opportunity to break out the matches and the petrol for a bonfire of red tape? To which I would respond that we have been there before. We have seen the impact that financial crises have in the real economy, how the fire spreads to affect real people. Real, if uneven, progress has been made in raising bank capital requirements to avoid that. At the same time, there is a clear global trend towards some level of transparency around asset ownership, driven by the pain to national exchequers of taxes forgone. Even Swiss banking secrecy is no longer absolute, at least if the US tax authorities are doing the asking. It is uncertain, to say the least, that the reinvention of London as a low-regulation centre is either possible or an outcome to be aspired to, and the idea that there is a majority for Brexit as a way to set the bankers free seems fanciful.

Others again will shrug and take comfort from the resilience of the City through the centuries. As so often in this context, an underlying truth, namely that the legal, tax and social environment of the UK has been propitious for service industries in general and the financial services industry particular, struggles to support a more grandiose notion that the UK is the lucky possessor an of innate national genius for dealing with other peoples' money. The proponents of this school of thought tend to ignore the quasi-accidental origins of London's recent hegemony, borne of a tax quirk that drove US Dollar debt capital raising from New York to London in the sixties. The fortunes of financial centres are not immutable.

And that is where we are. Discussion papers published by the pound (or kilo). A steady trickle of news stories around new office premises and the movement of a handful of employees, variously counted in the hundreds or thousands. Although a number of moves have been announced to Dublin, Luxembourg, and Paris, amongst others, the current is flowing most strongly across the

North Sea. Ironically, given the predilection on one side of the debate for 1940s-era metaphors, Frankfurt looks to be the big winner of the Brexit tug-of-war.

Why we are where we are

Moving is expensive, time-consuming and disruptive to businesses and the personal lives of employees. It is not something that companies will generally seek to do in the absence of a very good reason. Currently, the good reason is the increasing likelihood of a 'no-deal' exit. That in turn is driven by twin imperatives of process and time. Simply put, there is lot of the first and not very much at all of the second.

It was apparent from the outset that the UK political establishment under-estimated the importance of Brexit as a process. The European Commission is nothing if not a bureaucracy – otherwise known as a framework for getting stuff done in an organised fashion – and it was always going to approach Brexit as a rules-based exercise. That is not accidental – to do otherwise in a club of 28 countries would result in chaos. Beyond the Commission, the European Parliament, that imperfect but much-maligned institution, will assert its own role. UK governments of all stripes, operating to the universal principle that the perfect unit of management is your own, have never engaged with or recognised the Parliament as any sort of legitimate forum, and there may be a price to pay for that deficit of understanding. There are belated signs that the UK government may be taking the job seriously, but – to put it kindly –there is ground to make up here.

Process takes time. Over time, it is rational to assume that the laws of economic gravity will pull the economies of the UK and the remaining EU into some sort of relationship. But time is what we don't have, and that is a purely self-inflicted wound. We have always known that there is a two-year timeline to conclude discussions from the point at which the formal process of withdrawal is triggered. We have known also that a deal cannot be approved, or the timeline for negotiations extended, without the agreement of 27 remaining EU members and their various sub-polities, who may be variously disinterested, opportunistic or, just possibly, spiteful. And yet the UK government chose to give its formal notice of withdrawal in March 2017, immediately surrendering the negotiating advantage to its interlocutors.

Both the UK and the EU are, of course, committed exponents of the good-enough-for-now fudge, and that is certainly one possible future. But given the context and stakes, there must also be a high risk that exit will occur without agreement on the shape of the future relationship between the UK and the remaining EU – variously known as 'hard Brexit', 'clean Brexit' or, less optimistically, as the 'cliff-edge'.

And how we could be somewhere else

If we are seeking to pause or perhaps even reverse the implementation of Brexit exit plans, we would ideally reach for a solution that is comprehensive, yet capable of rapid implementation, requiring as little process, and therefore time, as possible. That seems to rule out any bespoke arrangement. There is in fact an off-the-peg model which might fit, although not one that I would have seen as a likely choice in those pre-Referendum discussions. In those conversations, we tended to heavily discount as an option continued membership of the European Economic Area (EEA) through membership of the European Free Trade Association (EFTA) – the so-called 'Norway option'. Other countries within the EEA but outside the EU are Iceland and Liechtenstein. The UK was a founder member of EFTA, before electing to join the EU and to begin its agonised national conversation with that body.

There were good reasons for viewing this as an unlikely outcome. The EEA exists in the penumbra of the EU proper and was originally conceived as an ante-chamber to membership. Membership involves continued contributions to EU funds, acceptance of EU rules in many contexts and the implementation of freedom of movement as a *quid pro quo* to the free movement of goods and services. EEA members are voteless, if not entirely without influence, in EU decisions. In other words, with perhaps one exception, EEA membership achieves none of the outcomes sought by ardent Brexiteers. The exception is that EEA members are not subject to the jurisdiction of the European Court of Justice (ECJ), typically seen as a key stumbling block in terms of sovereignty, the 'perhaps' is that they are subject to the jurisdiction of the EFTA Court, which will generally follow ECJ rulings in any event. On the other hand, EEA membership would in many respects leave the UK as a rule-taker than a rule-maker. There are particular challenges for financial services here, primarily relating to the delayed application of post-financial crisis regulation. Membership of EFTA is in the gift of the other members, and it is not certain that the UK would be welcome, in particular given that diplomacy appears, like the winning of football World Cups, to be a forgotten art in the UK.

And yet, as the reality of the national situation begins to hit home, it is worth re-visiting that initial conclusion. EEA membership would in many respect be a sensible staging post to exit. EEA members are outside the scope of EU rules in some highly sensitive areas such as agriculture and fisheries. EEA members are free to conclude free trade agreements elsewhere. Freedom of movement is more qualified than in the case of the full-fat EU option. Finally, critically, EEA membership would allow continued access to the onshore EU market which a no-deal exit will emphatically close. It would give those financial institutions and their equivalents in other industries which are currently expensively, laboriously, reluctantly implementing relocation plans significant pause for thought. The sheer heft of the UK's financial markets and the size and expertise of its regulator should provide some comfort that its views might continue to be influential.

Notwithstanding some public grumbling, EEA membership appears to function as stable end state for Norway. I would suggest that the same could be true of the UK. In many ways, it would capture the emotional register of the UK's relationship with the European mainland – transactional rather than romantic, in equal measure engaged and apart. Above all, it would be a neat summation of a divided nation if the end result of the referendum were an outcome which would fail to satisfy ideologues on either side, but would relegate issues of regulation and process to the small print where they belong, and perhaps in doing so allow the rest of the population to get on with their lives.

[i] Source: Key Facts about UK-based Financial and Related Professional Services, April 2017.
[ii] Source: Ditto.

The views expressed here are James Coiley's own.

The Conjuring

Catherine Coldstream

The bus we took was
Magic. Wrapped in
Donkey jackets we
Sat out the froth and foam
Of nights on the close edge of
Someone else's world,
In transit.

Coins in our pockets
were cold as pebbles
to our fingertips,
and rattled like old bones
along the threadbare hours,
slow time stretched and thrust forward
On fast spinning wheels.

Nights were black and white,
Crumpled as newsprint,
Damper than fish, more
Empty than a beer-stained glass.

While the world fled from us,
Cars and stars gone like gnats
Through reflective panes.

The port was all wetness
Tired bodies moving toward
Another plane. Aimless
Luggage stood silver-stretched
by lamplight, or on metal trollies,
Waiting to be conjured, claimed
And given purpose.

Mornings were full fat
Camembert, and rich
with languages and coffee
The clamorous coins in our pockets
Now less alien. I listened to
Ockeghem on my
Walkman.

One time I found a watch,
Made for a larger wrist than mine,
on the back seat, and the driver said
Keep it – after the announcement and the
Silence in the aisles that followed it.
It may come in handy. I
Should have laughed. We English
Are good at puns.

Instead I fitted it over my cold fingers,
Tips like pebbles, and felt it warm,
A slice of someone else's time
Under my donkey jacket.

And I was glad to belong here,
Stretched beyond spume, and
Magically no longer
On the other side.

DNA in three languages

Christine De Luca

DNA

Come siamo arrivati qui, in questo luogo,
quest'isola, con questa tribù? Molto probabile

che fossimo rintanati, cercando riparo
da cataclismi, dai venti più feroci,

da giorni senza sole, e notti senza stelle;
poi muovendo a nord nella caccia, svernando

per un'Era Glaciale, nella debole luce del fondo
delle caverne, dipingendo immagini di cervi,

di bisonti che battevano la strada, annusando un
sottile sentore di verde. Quando cedeva il freddo

noi ci siamo separati dalla nostra gente
siamo andati per la nostra strada, portando esche,

semi, e molti racconti; aprendo solchi dentro
una terra dura, pietrosa o intrisa d'acqua.

Nessuno è un'isola, ma noi siamo ancora
solitari, ambivalenti procreatori,

assuefatti alle barriere. C'è traccia, un rilevante
tratto dell'esploratore che permane nel DNA,

e ci mantiene in movimento, inostacolati;
unici, ma interrelati con l'intero mondo,

nel codice di quell'unico originario continente,
quella prima isola nell'oceano, la nostra genesi.

DNA

Foo wan we here, tae dis place,
dis island; an wi dis tribe? Laekly

we wir hunkered doon, hoidin
fae cataclysms, faercist winds,

fae sunless days, starnless nichts;
dan huntin wir wye nort, winterin

trowe a ice age, deep i da gloor
o caves, paintin eemages o deer,

o bison lunderin ahead, trackin a
niff o green. As caald slackent

we spleet fae wir ain fock,
gud wir gaet, kerryin tinderbox,

seeds, mony a tale; brakkin oot
a tyoch laand, steyney or sabbin.

Naeboady is a island, yet still wir
solitary, ambivalent begyetters,

wint wi boondaries. Der a hint, a gey
strynd o da explorer lingerin i da DNA,

keepin wis on da möv, untrammelled;
unique, but sib tae da hale wirld,

encodit i dat wan aerly continent,
dat first ocean island, wir genesis.

DNA

How did we get here, to this place,
this island; and with this tribe? Most likely

we were hunkered down, hiding
from cataclysms, fiercest winds,

from sunless days, starless nights;
then hunting our way north, wintering

through an Ice Age, deep in the faint light
of caves, painting images of deer,

of bison beating the ground ahead, tracking a
faint smell of green. As cold slackened

we split from our own people
went our way, carrying tinderbox,

seeds, many a tale; breaking out
a tough land, stony or waterlogged.

Nobody is an island, yet still we are
solitary, ambivalent begetters,

used to boundaries. There is a hint, a strong
trait of the explorer lingering in the DNA,

keeping us on the move, untrammelled;
unique, but related to the whole world,

encoded in that one early continent,
that first ocean island, our genesis.

In Answer

Uwe Derksen

Yanis Varoufakis had an article published in The Guardian on 3 May 2017, *The six Brexit traps that will defeat Theresa May*, in which he makes a number of claims and right from the start, reflecting on his own experience with the EU, he states: 'A little more than two years later, Theresa May is trying to arm herself with a clear democratic mandate ostensibly to bolster her negotiating position with European powerbrokers – including the German finance minister Wolfgang Schäuble – and to deliver the optimal Brexit deal.' His article, in many ways a good piece of analysis, gives us insight into the complicated relationship between democratic structure and Brussels' bureaucratic power. Yet, with the recent British general elections behind us, the phrase 'a clear democratic mandate' can appear far from clear. In fact , even before the general election, was it actually that clear? To my mind *vox populi* was, if anything, divided rather than clear. As ever the question is, do you test a population's desire during an atmosphere of crisis or during one of relative stability (though one may argue the case for an underlying permanent crisis in our societies)?

The 'Brussels machine' is not just a socialist phenomenon of large scale administration and central control as neoliberals like Margaret Thatcher liked to portray it (see her 'backdoor' Bruges speech in 1988 [i]) like many other large bureaucracies, the dynamics of power associated with such conglomerates and repeated attempts to subject them to efficient political control. Indeed, Britain was the playground for neoliberal ideas emulating the USA and pushing the glory of finance capital into an expanded Europe after the fall of the so-called 'iron curtain'. And people will recall the triumphalist gloating of the Anglo-American way of running, and by implication, the best way of managing the economy and how deregulation freed up the movement of capital paving the way into a 'free world'. People will also remember how the chapter of Anglo-American economic ideology ended. Yet, neither socialist nor capitalist bureaucracies function along democratic lines in any case. Bureaucracies maintain systems, they develop technical knowledge required for efficient process functions, they use power and subvert power by almost any means possible to defend the status quo or indeed to stay aligned with the most powerful. From the point of view of such bureaucracies, democratic scrutiny is a necessary evil in many societies. The idea that Westminster is not an administrative cartel for big industry – unlike Brussels – would be naïve, and that those countries with little power would be treated differently in any other union is wishful thinking.

I have yet to experience a bank that calls in the credit owed and asks the debtor to determine the premise of negotiation .

Bureaucratic and political power tango, and Germany is a good example. Its federated political structure, insisted upon by the British after the second world war (but only half-heartedly granted back home fifty years later to its constituent countries), served

Germany well, and helped to tackle though not root out completely its fascist cultural and psychological legacy over the years. It learned how to combine bureaucratic structures with democratically organised political power. Germany appears to be less worried about the Brussels bureaucracy than Britain is. Ah, one might point out, Germany comes from a position of political and economic might. For that matter, so does Britain. If there is a difference, and I speculate here based on my own experience, then it is rooted in different administrative cultures that set standards. Standards connect the technical (sort of value-free) with the wider cultural (value-laden) sentiment and by doing so help to drive particular narratives and imagery. In a world of global norms and measurements, these differences in standards are fast disappearing and can leave a cultural gap. An obvious example is the standardisation of language, where regional variances in pronunciation, terminologies used and even grammar have been lost by the introduction of a national standard and with it, local histories and identities. The British imperial standards made sense when its colonies needed efficient administration and control to allow effective fuelling of its industries, but I doubt that that world can be reinvented even if Theresa May in desperation looks at the Commonwealth again as an alternative to the EU. So she gets her lieutenants to preach the gospels of common values of the Commonwealth, *sic* standards: these were of course formerly imposed by Britain. The British find it difficult to break the circle so it seems.

I recall one of my teacher's (a right wing history teacher) excitement about the renaming of my secondary school in 1970s West-Germany: 'Europe school' was revealed to be the new name – why? 'because Europe is your future', he exclaimed passionately. I compare that experience with one I had some 20 years later, when myself and my colleagues were excited about running a number of EU projects involving students travelling to and from Spain, East Germany etc. In the process, we were trying to embed the EU Erasmus scheme at our college in Kent. We got a clear message from the principal at the time: 'Look at this carpet in my corridor, it is worn out because of those Erasmus students, there is no money in it for us, we are paying more than we get back.' In fact, in my professional life over the past 25 years plus I had many meetings set in a European context. In this regard, my British colleagues, especially anyone with some decision-making power or level of influence, be they from industry, government, education or politics, seemed to display a disingenuous attitude to the idea of Europe, in marked contrast to my colleagues from mainland Europe. This 'disingenuity' was not necessarily a deliberate or a fully conscious display of attitude and behaviour, but rather a symptom of an underlying cultural narrative of an unresolved new British identity which is somehow stifled within the wider European identity.

What are the positive cultural connectors' reference points that link the European culture with my own British culture? seemed to be the question they asked themselves subconsciously.

In fact, the distinction between Britain and mainland Europe is itself a symptom of that confused identity. The idea of Europe and Britain's role within it has a long history, and as such is not comparable to the Greek situation, but is rooted in a scenario in which a great political union of power gradually loses ground on the world stage because it it reluctant or unwilling to become part of another kind of union.

The narrative of being the imperial standard bearer in the world and not just Europe is deeply ingrained across the social and political spectrum and indeed British culture; one just needs to look at sport, the Arts, Britain's showcased culturally diverse communities. 'Britishness', or the British way of life and in its multifaceted interpretations has seeped into successive generations. In his valedictory despatch from the foreign service at the end of the 1970s, Sir Nicholas Henderson (who married a Greek woman) quoted Anthony Eden and his reference of January 1952, to the 'ideal' of European integration: 'This is something which we know, in our bones, we cannot do... For Britain's story and her interests lie beyond the continent of Europe. Our thoughts move across the seas...'[ii]. Margaret Thatcher's reluctance to support German unification, allegedly remarking 'we beat the Germans twice, and now they're back'[iii], is part of the underlying yet dominant sentiment. This imperialist language thus persists and was reclaimed and celebrated during the referendum but from a distance looks like the last twitches of a long drawn-out death.

'Brexit' (or 'Breakit' as I prefer to call it) is viewed first and foremost through a cultural lens (despite all the economic arguments); political and economic arguments are measured against British standards; whether these are real or have become illusionary (a Freudian wish) is of little relevance here. With the growth of globalised capital, bureaucracies will grow too. It remains to be seen whether the old cultural cloak will be ripped open and replaced or whether the 'Brexiteers' can get to work fast enough to tailor the necessary alterations to make it fit. As far as bureaucracies are concerned, they will always have the last laugh as long as there is a standard...

[i] Margaret Thatcher's Bruges speech 1988 transcript:
https://www.margaretthatcher.org/document/107332
[ii] Sir Nicolas Henderson speech in The Economist, 2 June 1979
[iii] Der Spiegel, 11 September 2009

One Year On from the Brexit Referendum

Michael Dougan

It's just over a year since the government endorsed the narrow victory of the Leave alliance in the 2016 referendum on UK membership of the EU.

Now that events have finally begun to move, there is an enormous amount of work for constitutional lawyers, like me, to get our teeth into. Obviously, myself and my colleagues are now engaged in detailed analysis of developments such as the ongoing withdrawal negotiations and the so-called Repeal Bill. But a lot of people have been asking for a more general review, simply of where things have got to 'one year on'.

For those purposes, I went back to a lecture I gave in Liverpool last June – only a matter of days before the referendum itself – in which I described the Leave campaign as being guilty of dishonesty on an industrial scale. But just as importantly, in that lecture, I also identified what any competent constitutional lawyer could have safely foreseen as the likely consequences of a Leave victory in the referendum.

Such concerns were dismissed by Leave campaigners as a lawyer's version of 'Project Fear'. But what is striking is how things are unfolding pretty much as expected.

In particular: I made four sets of predictions: two relating to the internal challenges that would face the UK; and two related to the external tasks that we would have to confront.

The first prediction was that a vote to leave would trigger a comprehensive review of the entire legal system, which would be needed to prepare the UK for withdrawal: after all, for over 40 years, UK law has evolved under the influence of and in combination with EU law. The impact of EU law may well vary from sector to sector, but such is the nature of EU membership that trying to divide 'national law' from 'European law' is more a task for philosophers than for lawyers or civil servants.

Moreover: the sheer scale and complexity of that review would inevitably entail a massive delegation of power from parliament to the government: it was simply impossible to imagine how such a vast job could be done by parliament itself.

And more generally: leaving the EU would also remove the regulatory safety nets provided by EU law, that prevent any government minded to do so from deregulating basic protections for workers and the environment and consumers etc.

So: Project Fear or Project Reality?

The government has now published both a White Paper and a draft legislative text on the so-called Repeal Bill. It recognises the urgent need to prepare the UK legal system for withdrawal, which would otherwise cause tremendous uncertainty and dislocation. For that purpose: the government proposes to incorporate all existing EU law directly into the UK legal system, so as to minimise disruption and ensure continuity. But the government also recognises that a lot of EU law doesn't actually make much sense if you're no longer a Member State: for example, where EU law seeks to solve cross-border problems by coordinating the activities of different national authorities.

And so the government agrees: the UK needs to carry out a comprehensive review of the entire legal system, just to prepare the UK for withdrawal; and that review will need to adapt and in many cases replace existing EU rules with some workable UK alternative. That job cannot realistically be done by Parliament alone – so the government is demanding wide-ranging and far-reaching powers for itself to change the existing law. Make no mistake: not only does this legislation raise all sorts of more detailed technical questions, for example, about which parts of EU law the government proposes to incorporate and which to reject. It also poses very serious questions about our constitutional fundamentals – executive scrutiny, democracy and legitimacy.

In any case: in some sectors, even the government recognises that the scale of the changes will be so extreme that Parliament itself will need to work through a major programme of primary legislation, aimed at rewriting the regulatory regimes applicable to whole fields of our economy and society. The Queen's Speech from June 2017 lists several such fields: e.g. customs, agriculture, fisheries, immigration, and trade. Only trifling matters, obviously.

The amount of time and resource that will be spent just on preventing the country experiencing regulatory and administrative malfunction is astounding. But in the meantime: we should pay careful attention to the gathering 'anti-red tape' campaigns – being promoting by the likes of the Daily Telegraph – which seek to portray withdrawal as some 'once in a lifetime opportunity' to sweep away any number of EU-derived rights and obligations. To them, of course, 'red tape' means our rights as workers and consumers, or the regulatory standards intended to protect the environment or our broader safety and security as citizens. And don't forget: short term promises in party manifestos to 'protect workers rights' count for very little – leaving the EU is about imposing a long term, structural change in our social contract with public power.

That all sounds like Project Reality to me.

Our second prediction was that a vote to leave could lead to radical changes in the constitutional structure of the UK. For example: it could increase the likelihood of a second referendum on Scottish independence. And it could create serious problems for Northern Ireland, not least through a hardening of the border with the Republic.

Project Fear or Project Reality?

Before the general election, the Scottish government, with the support of the Scottish Parliament, formally requested permission to hold a second independence referendum. Since the election, the First Minister has postponed plans for holding a second referendum, at least until the nature of any UK-EU deal becomes clearer. But in the meantime: the devolved administrations continue to lament an almost complete lack of serious engagement with their concerns by the government in London. Whatever happens in due course: the political damage done to relations between Edinburgh and Westminster is very serious.

And the Repeal Bill may well only make the tensions worse: although the government insists that it expects withdrawal from the EU to lead (over some unidentified timescale) to greater powers for the devolved administrations, it has laid down only very vague criteria, aimed primarily at justifying the centralisation of power in London – such as preserving the UK single market and enabling the UK to enter into international trade agreements. There is little sign of any countervailing constitutional mechanisms – such as a domestic equivalent of the principle of subsidiarity – to protect the interests of the devolved regions.

As for Northern Ireland: there is now at least broad consensus among responsible actors that this is the region of the UK that stands to be most damaged by withdrawal. The border problems in particular are very real – especially in the field of customs; indeed, they are now considered top of the agenda for negotiations with the EU. And political tensions have not been helped by the minority Conservative government's deal with the hard right DUP – a deal which, even on a generous interpretation, devalues the 'honest broker' principle which is meant to facilitate the smooth operation of the Good Friday settlement.

Again: that all sounds like Project Reality to me.

Our third prediction concerned relations with the EU. In particular, we suggested that there would be negotiations on an agreement dealing with the mechanics of withdrawal (e.g. migrant rights); then separately, the possibility of a framework agreement on future relations (particularly in the field of trade). But the latter agreement could only be concluded after we had already left the EU and was likely to take far longer than two years to finalise. In the meantime: we might be forced to trade under the minimalist rules of the WTO – a scenario which every credible commentator regards as deeply unsatisfactory if not deeply damaging.

Project Fear or Project Reality?

What amazes me here, is how many Leave campaigners – within government as well as outside it – are still living in a state of almost total denial about what is happening.

In assessing the PM's decision to call a general election – the UK's negotiating position was seriously flawed from the outset, by the government's rather fantastical demand that all negotiations with the EU – on the mechanics of withdrawal, on a broad and ambitious future relationship, and on appropriate transitional arrangements – all of it should be done and dusted within a timescale of about 18 months.

By contrast, the EU's consistent approach was always both more legally robust and more practically realistic: first, we sort out the mechanics of withdrawal; then, given sufficient progress, we can start preliminary and preparatory discussions about the future; but that future relationship can only be progressed after the UK has already left – and it is likely to take a lot longer to conclude.

David Davies had promised to make this the 'row of the summer'. But of course, now that negotiations are actually underway, the inevitable has happened: the EU position is simply being imposed upon the UK –like it or not. So much for 'taking back control'.

So far, the negotiations, just on the mechanics of withdrawal, have already thrown up some obvious points of tension. For example: despite the PM's rhetoric about guaranteeing citizens' rights, and not using them as bargaining chips, the UK baffled many of the other member states by refusing to match (by quite some considerable distance) the EU's existing offer of a full and reciprocal safeguard for the existing rights of all current migrants. Meanwhile, Tory Europhobes continue their strategy of seeking to whip up tabloid hysteria at any prospect of a financial settlement of the UK's rights and liabilities – no doubt having identified this as their best chance to sabotage the chances of securing any withdrawal deal at all. Though to be fair, the government isn't doing too bad a job of that for itself: just look at their frankly irrational hatred of the European Court of Justice – as distorted and dishonest as anything else in the Leave campaign – which is nevertheless effectively dictating much of the UK's future relations with the EU.

If the current negotiations on the mechanics of withdrawal are already at risk of getting bogged down, if not derailed, then any future negotiations towards a framework agreement, covering issues such as trade, security and defence, remain at such a level of sketchiness that they could qualify as work of abstract art. On virtually every single major issue one would expect to address in any significant trade or cooperation agreement, when it comes to the UK's vision and preferences, we know almost nothing.

For now, the government is sticking to its White Paper from February 2017. Which means we will be leaving the EU customs union. Instead, we want a special relationship with the customs union – it's just that we can't say yet what that might mean. And we will be leaving the single market (even as members of the European Economic Area). Instead, we want a special relationship with the single market – it's just that we can't say yet what that might mean. All we do know is: the government doesn't want the free movement of natural persons; and rejects the jurisdiction of the Court of Justice. They show almost no awareness of the price to be paid for those 'red lines'. But that's almost irrelevant – since we don't currently have any credible position on any other matter either. And let's not pretend that the attitude of the Labour Party in opposition is much better: it isn't.

This almost complete lack of detail from Britain's political leaders is all the more striking, when one bears in mind several crucially important contextual factors:

First, the UK cannot simply wish away the inherent problems of international trade; especially the challenge of tackling non-tariff (regulatory) barriers to cross border trade in goods and services. Leading

Leave campaigners and indeed government ministers seem oblivious to the real difficulties in securing better trade terms between developed economies. And particularly when it comes to provision of services, the UK will be seeking an entirely novel deal, with no clear international precedents.

Secondly, the UK is not seeking to improve trading conditions with the EU; it is seeking to minimise the mutual loss of market access. In less than two years' time, the regulatory conditions for UK companies doing business across Europe (and vice versa) are set to become substantially less favourable than they are now – actively creating a vast array of barriers to trade, which (at best) will increase costs and (at worst) will seal off markets, either in law or in fact.

Thirdly, and as the European Council has repeatedly affirmed: no relationship, no matter how close, can offer the same benefits as EU membership. If the UK wants privileged access to the single market, it has to sign up to the EU's expectations on regulatory standards and enforcement – and not just now, but into the future as well. The EU will insist on a level playing field, e.g. in fields such as competition and state aid. It will safeguard against unfair competitive advantages, e.g. as regards tax, social and environmental dumping. And the UK will pay for such privileges – just like everyone else has to.

Project Fear? Actually, it all sounds like Project Reality to me.

Our fourth and final set of predictions was that, when it comes to relations with the rest of the world, we would face a series of challenges: 1) the loss of our existing trade agreements (dozens of them) as already negotiated by the EU; 2) the need urgently to build capacity in the highly specialist and complex field of international trade negotiations and representation; 3) the likelihood that our bargaining power on the international scene will prove to be significantly more limited than it is as part of the single market; and 4) the risk that other countries would expect clarity about our domestic and regional trade position before entering advanced talks on new trade deals.

To be fair, it is still a little too early to tell just yet, exactly how this prediction will pan out. But perhaps we have enough little signs already to know the general direction of travel.

E.g. we know that the EU will indeed regard us as being excluded, upon withdrawal, from existing deals negotiated by the EU for the benefit of its member states.

E.g. several countries have expressed their interest in a future trade deal with the UK in principle; but in practice, they intend to prioritise their own economic relations with the EU and (by the way) would prefer us to clarify our position first please.

By contrast, the government treats every random statement about some great, very powerful, very quick trade deal, uttered from the mouth or keyboard of the terrifyingly unstable President Trump, as if it were gospel – conveniently forgetting that Trump has been absolutely consistent about just one aspect of US international relations: America First.

Indeed, the contrast between the government's haughty arrogance towards the EU and its obsequious desperation towards America hardly bodes well for our negotiating skill and credibility. Especially against the worrying background of a government which has repeatedly threatened, that the reality of 'Global Britain' could mean competing on world markets as some sort of low tax, low regulation – and with it low productivity, low public services – sweatshop economy. Let's hope that the so-called left wing leavers feel proud of helping sweep a hard right movement to power and giving it the constitutional leeway it needs to realise its hard right objectives.

The basic reality is that, whatever the delusions of the leave campaigners, we are now firmly on course to discover that even we – the British – are not exempt from two principles that are simply axiomatic to international trade relations.

First, the ambition of an international trade agreement is conditioned primarily by the willingness of the parties to agree ambitious regulatory frameworks and sophisticated institutional arrangements, that will help promote mutual trust between their respective political, administrative and judicial authorities. The more ambitious the deal, the more extensive the obligations, and the more extensive the obligations, the more your theoretical national autonomy is constrained in practice.

Secondly, in international trade, size matters: the bigger players dictate the rules of the game. They do so at the global level: the key international organisations which develop the rules of the world economy are (like it or not) dominated by the interests of the US and the EU, increasingly China. The same is true at the bilateral level: the EU determines the terms on which smaller economies can better access its market; if those smaller countries are not willing to pay the price, they don't get the better access.

So: looking back, one year on, it seems that events are unfolding in a way that was entirely predictable and indeed actively predicted.

One of the key roles of a constitutional lawyer is to help ensure that those who exercise (or who seek to exercise) public power are held accountable for their actions. In the context of the UK's withdrawal from the EU, you might think that that job has in some respects been made easier. After all, Leave campaigners are in the process of becoming subject to a form of accountability they have never really had to experience before: the accountability of reality. The time has come when their fantasies have to find solutions to real problems; they have to negotiate with people who haven't been conned into sharing their distorted worldview; they have to address challenges which they denied would ever even materialise.

But how will they respond? By welcoming the scrutiny? By admitting their mistakes? By apologising for their reckless risktaking? Of course. They'll ignore, they'll deny, they'll blame everyone else except themselves – the internal saboteurs and the spiteful foreigners. And it's that which actually makes the challenge of accountability more difficult and yet also more important: our job is to help ensure that Leave campaigners are held responsible for the consequences of their own choices and actions, judged against their own promises and denials.

The Levellers and the Diggers: the Original Eurosceptics

Giles Fraser

I can still picture Billy Bragg standing on that stage, giving it full-throated fire and moral defiance. You probably know the lyrics (by Leon Rosselson):

'In 1649, to St George's Hill,
A ragged band they called the Diggers
Came to show the people's will.
They defied the landlords.
They defied the laws.
They were the dispossessed
Reclaiming what was theirs.'

What most people know about the Diggers and their leader Gerard Winstanley was that they were religious socialists who wanted to turn the land into a common treasury. What they often don't know is that they were also Eurosceptics. So Winstanley begins his book, *The True Levellers Standard Advanced*, also written in 1649: 'O what mighty Delusion, do you, who are the powers of England live in!

That while you pretend to throw down that Norman yoke, and Babylonish power, and have promised to make the groaning people of England a Free People; yet you still lift up that Norman yoke, and slavish Tyranny, and holds the People as much in bondage, as the Bastard Conquerour himself, and his Councel of War.'

I am no great fan of nationalism. And I want us to welcome far more refugees into this country, not less – they are fleeing a slavish Tyranny and Councel of War, after all. But, nonetheless, I believe in people's democracy and so I will be voting for us to leave the European Union. For Winstanley, the Norman yoke went back to the invasion of 1066 and William the Conqueror, who set his French nobleman over the English peasantry, thus generating centuries of resentment against foreign rule. The kings and nobles may have learned to speak English over time, but they were still an alien power imposed without popular consent. This is why the Levellers, who met in my old church in Putney, first demanded democracy as a way to curb the imposition of heteronomous power, power imposed from without, from a distance.

In the 16th century, Henry VIII had broken with Rome and established home rule for the church. As article 37 of the 39 articles puts it: 'The bishop of Rome hath no jurisdiction in this realm of England.' The Bible was to be written in English and not in a foreign language that ordinary people could not understand. In the 17th century, the monarchy itself was deposed, Charles I being regularly depicted as a reincarnation of 'the Bastard Conquerour himself'. In the popular imagination, the English Reformation was a Brexit.

All of which is why someone like Tony Benn was such a prominent Eurosceptic. Steeped in the history of 17th-century radicalism, Benn knew that democracy was about the power of the people. 'It's not for members of parliament to give away the powers that were lent to them because they don't belong to members of parliament, they belong to the electorate,' argued Benn, yet 'we live in a continent where increasingly power has gone to a group of people who are not elected, cannot be removed and don't have to listen to us.' The point is not that we don't want to be beholden to foreigners but that power must stay close to the people from which it flows. The more distant the power, the more faceless and bureaucratic, the less its legitimacy. We now cast more votes for Big Brother than we do for Europe's politicians.

No, the bastard conqueror isn't the European Union – we freely gave the powers away. But the EU has meekly become his servant. The bastard conqueror is international finance that ignores borders, locates itself offshore to pay no tax, and has the EU in its pocket. Look at how the EU dealt with Greece, imposing crippling austerity on its people. Look at the Transatlantic Trade and Investment Partnership, the massive trade deal that the EU has been negotiating – mostly in secret – with the US. Under the terms of this deal, large companies will be able to sue nation states if they introduce policies that curb its profits. I'd vote against TTIP if I could. But because of the way the EU is negotiating the deal, I have no say in the matter. And nor do you. The EU has become a neoliberal club, and I will not worship the God they serve.

'Was the Earth made to preserve a few covetous, proud men to live at ease, and for them to bag and barn up the treasures of the Earth from others, that these may beg and starve in a fruitful land; or was it make to preserve all her children?' said Winstanley. Now that would be a common agricultural policy worth voting for.

I Won't Miss EU

Rick Garboil

I won't miss you France, with your smelly cheese,
or Cyprus with your myrtle trees.
I won't miss you Spain, with your flamenco,
or Italy with your pizza dough.

Finland, miss you? No! No fear,
nor Denmark, with your well-known beer.
Romania? You've got Castle Dracula,
and I hear the scenery's quite spectacular.

I won't miss Hungary, or its spas,
or Germany's reliable cars.
Greece is the word, well no, it's not.
And as for Malta, small hot rock!

Latvia has Art Nouveau,
but tell me, did *you* ever go?
And if you travel with a mania,
would you visit Lithuania?

Poland gave us Madame Curie,
Nobel laureate, Chemist, sure she
coined the term 'radioactivity'
but miss Poland? I've no proclivity.

The hills are alive in Austria,
but I won't miss them, no, I'm sure.
Another place I've been but seldom,
moules-frites? I won't miss you, Belgium.

The Netherlands has lots of bikes,
they clog the streets, but clogs and dykes
are not the things I'm bound to miss
from a low-lying land at a time like this.

And heck, I'm not about to be sick
pining for the Czech Republic.
Most castles and chateaux per capita,
but miss you? No, I won't, Slovakia.

Sweden, you gave us Ikea and Abba,
you've made my life a whole lot fabber,
but you're quite far north, in fact you're only a
stone's throw from Tallinn, Estonia.

I don't think the world will get any scarier
if I plan not to miss you either, Bulgaria.
I love your choral folk tradition
but missing you is not my mission.

From Cork City my granny came
but miss you Ireland? You're insane
if you think I'm going to miss your craic
on a two-way visit (there and back).

Unlike the alien acacia
I've not been widespread in Croatia.
But if I have a place to pick
I won't miss lovely Dubrovnik.

I've not been slumberous in Slovenia,
but how can I sleep when I've never been there?
And as for my final port of call?
No way I'll miss you, Portugal.

No I won't miss you, one and all,
all twenty-seven, not at all!
The countries I've already seen,
the countries where I've never been.

Because come what may
(I don't mean Theresa)
I would never
vote to leave yer.

No matter how we break our union,
for me there's never been confusion.
Strangers, foreigners, no, you bet,
just lots of friends I've not yet met.

So I'll go again to places been
I'll plan some trips to those not seen.
I was, I am, I'll always be an
enthusiastic European.

My European Family

Cecilia Hall

My family origins, at least the ones I know about, stretch from Slovenia and Austria in the east, to Portugal in the west, and from south to north from southern Italy to Scotland and Ireland (and probably Scandinavia). I am married to an Englishman so my children combine my mainly Scottish-Italian ancestry with English (as far as he knows).

My sisters and I exist because of the Second World War; without it our parents would never have met, and it is ironic that a war which was fought as a result of terrible racism and extreme nationalism should have ended up bringing so many people together of different nationalities and cultures who otherwise would never have found one another. My mother's family were Italian by nationality, but unlike so many Italians who relate back to a 'paese' in some specific region in Italy, they were in fact from all over, having moved around for a variety of reasons through the generations. My mother's father was from an Italian expatriate family who had settled in Egypt for several generations – they were involved in banking and money exchange, as was my grandfather; a previous member of his family had been a financial adviser to the King of Egypt at the time of the construction of the

Suez Canal. There was a very large Italian community in Egypt before World War Two, large enough to support the publishing of an Italian language daily newspaper, although the main language spoken by European expatriates of all nationalities was French.

My Italian grandmother, on the other hand, came from a family which had moved around a great deal within Italy. Her father was a cavalry officer in the Italian army whose family (the Cialente) were from L'Aquila, in Abruzzo. His military career meant that my grandmother's youth was spent constantly moving to different towns in Italy, wherever he happened to be posted, and also in Trieste, where her mother was from. So my grandmother was a mix of northern and southern Italian; at the time of her birth, in 1898, her father happened to be posted to Cagliari, in Sardinia, so she was born there, though her brother, who was only two years older, was born in Treviglio, in Lombardy. The family went on to live in Rome, Florence, Genoa and Milan. Her mother was from an Austrian-Italian/Slovene family which had settled in Trieste and had become increasingly italianised over the generations. My grandmother, Fausta Cialente, an Italian novelist, wrote a book about their complicated history *Le Quattro Ragazze Wieselberger* which is an account of their family origins as it relates to Trieste's history and the irredentist feelings which made them long to unite with Italy. A previous member of the family had made money as a merchant in Trieste (a very important port for the Habsburg Empire) thus freeing my great great-grandfather Gustavo Wieselberger to devote himself to music as a teacher, composer and conductor.

The family, who spoke both German and Italian, were very musical and my great-grandmother was thought talented enough to be sent to Bologna to study opera and to train as a singer, unusual at that time for her class and generation. After an operatic performance in which she sang a leading part, she was introduced by a mutual friend to a handsome young Abruzzese cavalry officer, and they very quickly fell in love and married. Though not at all a happy marriage, it produced two very talented children: my grandmother, who became a prize-winning novelist and noted journalist, and my great-uncle Renato Cialente, an actor with his own company who also worked with many of the leading film directors and actors of the day, including Vittorio de Sica. Sadly, I never met him as he was run over and killed by a Nazi truck during Rome's blackout in 1943; whether this was deliberate or accidental was was never known.

Perhaps it was in order to get away from her tyrannical father that my grandmother Fausta married a man more than twenty years older than herself, my grandfather Enrico Terni. They met in Italy, perhaps through a family connection, though he lived, worked and had been born in Egypt. They were married in Fiume in 1921, then a disputed part of Italy, and now known as Rijeka in Croatia. They went to live in Alexandria in Egypt, where my mother was born in 1923. My grandparents Enrico and Fausta were outspoken anti-fascists, and Fausta, who was already a published writer be fore the war, and a journalist, worked with the British authorities in Cairo during WW2 to make anti-fascist broadcasts intended to reach Italian POW's in Egypt and any other Italians who could pick up Radio Cairo as it was then known. 'Siamo Italiani, parliamo agli Italiani...' My grandparents were part of a group of expatriate Europeans who were deeply opposed to fascism and Nazism and though they certainly did not share British imperialist ideals or ambitions (still very prevalent within the senior officer class of the day) made common cause with the British in the desperate fight against the Axis powers, a fight that then, of course they were not to know would eventually be won. They would lay on parties and entertainments for British seamen when they had shore leave in Alexandria, and this is how my British father and Italian mother met. When they first met my father knew no Italian and my mother knew very little English; the only language they had in common was French and so their first letters to one another were in French. Recently I read my father's letters to my mother and her parents, (with whom he had become great friends) which he wrote from his ship (he was stationed in the Mediterranean as a young officer for most of the war) and I am astonished how quickly he learned to speak and write in Italian and also by how fast my mother learned to do the same in English. They were highly motivated of course.

Before the war my father, John Muir, who was born in Delhi in 1918, had been reading Modern Languages at university, specifically German and French. He was a natural linguist – having been born in India from a long line of Scottish orientalists and civil servants – and he always said that his first language was Hindi as in infancy he had been handed over to an Indian ayah since his mother was not at all maternal. As part of his modern languages degree he had spent time in both France and Germany; he was in Germany in 1938 and with first-hand knowledge of that country firmly in the grip of Nazism, came home convinced that war was inevitable. He decided to volunteer because that way you were able to choose which of the forces you would join; he was determined to join the Navy as he had already had some sea-going experience and knew how to navigate, which is why he became an officer so young. After an initial year in destroyers north of the Arctic Circle, off Norway, he was given the command of an MTB (Motor Torpedo Boat) in the Mediterranean. People were given responsibility so young in those desperate times; the missions he and his able seamen had to go on were very dangerous and not surprisingly he had periods of doubting if he really was up to skippering an MTB. My mother's family and their home in Alexandria were a haven for him and he and my mother realised quite early on that they were very serious about each other; despite the very special circumstances in which they had met, they decided to become engaged quite early on during the war. In fact, they longed to get married, but realised that that would be unwise given the danger my father was in on his many missions, and like many others at the time I think, he didn't want her to be made an instant widow. His by then retired parents had been living for some time in the UK and in his frequent letters home he had let them know about his friendship with the Terni family, his engagement to my mother Lionella, and their intention to marry. Sadly, many years living in India had left his parents psychologically isolated and they had found it difficult to settle down to country life in the North Riding where my grandfather had tried farming and bee-keeping. Their attitude to my father's proposed marriage was wholly negative, to the point of writing to my mother, who of course they had never met, to try to dissuade her. Fortunately my parents were not put off, and they had a very simple wedding ceremony at the British Consulate in Alexandria in October 1945 with only Fausta and Enrico, and a few friends present. My mother wore a very modern-looking 1940s suit with a nipped-in jacket, shoulder pads and a knee-length skirt; (no frothy white dress for her) and she looked wonderful.

After he was demobbed, my father took my mother to the UK to meet his family as soon as he could; I think he hoped they would be converted upon meeting her. His elderly aunt travelled all the way from Edinburgh to meet my mother at Tilbury; she was one of three of his father's sisters, two of whom, Kitty and Edie, lived together in Edinburgh; they adored my father, having no children of their own, and Aunt Edie wanted to give my mother the warmest possible welcome to the UK. This was not the welcome my mother received upon her arrival in north Yorkshire; she faced a chilly reception and I have been told by friends of the family, as well as by my mother herself, that my grandmother Gwladys simply refused to speak to her. My grandfather once commented that her piano playing was lovely, but that was one of the few kind things ever said, and when later on, we were taken as small children to visit, we were almost entirely ignored by our UK grandparents. It was good of my father to take the trouble to visit his elderly parents at all, and to try to help them to get to know their only grandchildren, because in the interim they had told him not to expect a penny from them and that he had been definitively cut out of their will. And all because, while fighting for his (and their) country, he had had the temerity to meet, fall in love with and marry a lovely young Italian woman. I know that they regarded me and my sisters as not really British – as mongrels at best – and when last year the referendum on EU membership was narrowly won by the Leave faction to me it felt like the hurt and rejection my family had experienced was writ large and anew.

Towards the end of the war because my father was so good at languages and had such an open, and inclusive attitude to people of all nationalities, he had wanted to become a liaison officer in the post-war reconstruction period. In fact he joined the British Council, and because of his Italian connections was posted to Milan (still in ruins) and to Rome in the immediate post-war period; later he was sent to a British Council regional office in Leeds, where I was born. When I was a few months old he was sent to Lebanon for a year to follow an intensive course in Arabic for diplomats and journalists who would be posted throughout the Middle East. My mother found herself in the Arab world once more, and most of my childhood and adolescence were spent between Syria, Kuwait and Iraq. I have wonderful memories of those countries, and feel great sadness at what has happened to them since. We always spent our summers in north Italy, which is where my grandmother was living by then, and learned to speak Italian in the few short weeks we were there each year. In between, and later, my parents lived and worked in first Portugal and then Spain, and we got to know those beautiful countries well. Both my parents were true internationalists and were wholly in favour of Britain's membership of the EEC, later the EU; if they had still been alive for last year's referendum they would undoubtedly have been appalled by the result. I still hope that in time this country will come to realise that its best interests lie in staying in. My father was so keen on European unity that he bought shares in the Channel Tunnel; unfortunately he didn't live to see it operational. I wonder if such an ambitious engineering project would even be built now, so we can perhaps be grateful that it was constructed when it was. We in Europe have enjoyed over seventy years of peace because of our countries' (not always easy or necessarily entirely successful) attempts to co-operate, after the most terrible war in which millions died, and for which my parents' generation gave up their youth. Narrow nationalism seems everywhere to be rearing its ugly head once more but we would all do well to remember that what unites us is stronger than what divides us, and what divides us is quite superficial.

I wanted to write about my European family because I, like many people, feel absolutely European, British and Italian, and not in any particular order.

My sources, apart from family conversations, are my parents' and grandparents' wartime correspondence, my grandmother Fausta Cialente's novel, already referred to, and her Diario di Guerra documenting her years as a journalist and broadcaster in Egypt, held at the Fondo Manoscritti at the University of Pavia.

Nous les européens

Andrea Inglese

On se porte assez bien
on n'a pas perdu pied
on a encore des idées, des mots à dire
on est bourré de projets, on est à fond dans l'invention
on déplace des choses, on élargit l'esprit

nous les européens, les gens nous détestent

moi je ne la maitrise pas très bien cette formule «nous les
    européens»
bien sûr je conçois l'urgence, la nécessité de l'époque
il faut s'y mettre, «nous les européens», au début
ça sonne bizarre, mais je m'accroche, par sentiment
de responsabilité, «nous les européens, on est pas
encore mort, on tient la position, on est là
dans la bonne vieille Europe»
je veux bien le dire, mais les gens ne nous supportent pas

on les énerve
ils veulent nous aplatir avec les camions, les fourgonnettes,
     ils flinguent
il a y du malentendu de civilisation, et ça nous coute cher
en caméras de surveillance

les gens expérimentés, pourtant, disent qu'on a bien fait
     les choses
on peut être fier, la vieille Europe n'est pas si vielle
elle se modernise tout le temps, se peaufine
on est souple, on a beaucoup de tolérance
tout ce qu'on peut tolérer chez nous!
mais c'est les gens qui ne nous tolèrent plus
(moi je voudrais le devenir
avant d'être exécuté à la bonbonne de gaz
un européen tolérant)

je vois bien qu'être italien ou français ne sert plus à grande chose
qu'il faut faire face à la compétition mondiale
avec une armure morale et politique d'européen
mais il faut s'y connaitre en histoire-géo, ce n'est pas innée
d'être un bon européen

j'espère en tout cas que si l'Europe existe
elle a un corps suffisamment compact et homogène
pour que je puisse m'y glisser dedans, un corps
sans failles, judéo chrétien mais éclairé
jusqu'au libéralisme

mais on ne peut pas toujours être aimés, même les nôtres
nous détestent, les plus jeunes des nôtres, il leur fallait
plus d'histoire et géographie, le respect
de l'orthographe

nous ne pouvons pas être si mauvais au fond
avec toutes les églises qu'on a construit
pendant des siècles rien que des magnifiques églises
des cathédrales des œuvres
de pitié en pierre et marbre
et le jugement d'Hippocrate
et l'Encyclopédie
nous on s'est toujours soucié de l'humanité, de l'humanité totale,
    entière
nous en avons trop fait parfois, c'est possible

mais la géo avant tout, les bons cours de géo en primaire, au
    collège
avec la carte de l'Europe toute déployée sur le mur face à nous
l'Europe derrière le bureau comme un paysage abstrait, monotone
qui s'anime et grouille de personnages mystérieux dès qu'on
    approche
dès qu'on lui pointe le nez dessus : les cercles frêles des villages
    perdus, les traits
tremblants et fins des rivières secondaires, les îles anonymes,
    morceaux
de terre flottante sans raison loin des côtes, de près cette Europe
partait dans tous les sens, on y cherchait bien une limite, un
    contour
rassurant, pour qu'elle soit comme de la chair mise sous boyau
une saucisse bien ferme de peuples et territoires, mais on
    comprenait jamais
la limite, sur la droite, à l'est, elle s'arrêtait où notre maison
    commune?
à la Russie ou à l'Union Soviétique? mon regard glissait toujours
au de là des Monts Oural, poussé vers le couloir illimité, le grand
réservoir d'espace: l'épouvantable Sibérie, on pouvait se tenir tout

au nord

proche du cercle arctique, partant par Arkhangelsk, jamais loin de
la mer

ou au contraire tracer un chemin au milieu, jusqu'au village de
Tobolsk

avant de foncer de manière abrupte sur la marge de la carte, là

la Sibérie disparaissait et le mur de la classe revenait, sale, idiot

sans l'éclat de la toponymie, et à cause de ça

on ne savait jamais où commençait l'Asie où terminait l'Europe

et qu'est ce qu'était au juste la grande chose soviétique, amorphe

et fascinante, qui flottait au milieu

de ce coté-là, de toute manière, la limite n'était pas étanche

la frontière ouest par contre, on nous avait dit, elle n'avait pas de
mystères:

Espagne et Portugal, puis l'océan, toute une surface bleu qui
sépare

mais encore une fois j'étais moi poussé par une diagonale
ascendante

j'avais une envie folle d'aller à Reykjavik, loin de tout, dans une
île

où on parlait une langue peu probable, installée à la limite de la
carte

vers ce nord absolu qui ne manifestait plus aucun point de repère

ce nord qui avait vaincu l'obstination méticuleuse des
cartographes

ils ne dessinaient plus presque rien, de simples contours, on ne
savait pas

si c'était la mer, la terre, la glace ou quelque chose d'autre, d'une
matière différente

mais là encore les comptes n'étaient pas justes, on nous avait privé

par amputation silencieuse, du Groenland, question d'économie
d'espaces

sans doute, mais on brouillait encore une fois les pistes, et je vois
mal

ici, après la découpe du règne de Danemark, cette «finesse de
sentiment

moral», dont parle Renan, propre à nous, les indo-européens, les
ariens

où serait-elle notre «morbidesse» proverbiale, face à ce geste de
boucher

qui veut démêler une frontière occidentale pas du tout évidente

pour l'avoir facile sur la carte, à plat, nette et propre, l'Europe

mais ce n'est pas qu'un territoire, l'Europe, une affaire de
frontières

ou de bassins hydrographiques, je suis d'accord, c'est un mot
aussi

une chose symbolique, un sentiment profond, toute une histoire

des milliards d'année de culture, j'exagère, des millions,

quelques centaines d'années au moins, il faut se mettre

en mode souvenir : et déjà je me rappelle de Rubens

Pierre Paul, vigueur et raffinement, il n'y a pas de plus européen

mais immédiatement c'est l'autre qui me vient à l'esprit

de six ans plus jeune, la pourriture von Wallenstein Albrecht

le condottiere, ils surgissent par couples, le peintre-diplomate

et le générale-entrepreneur, le sommet de la peinture baroque

et la machine à pillage et massacre de la guerre de Trente ans

il ne faut pas s'assombrir, mais si j'évoque Wittgenstein Ludwig

le plus radical et vagabond des philosophes du siècle passé

il traine avec lui l'autre, le peintre raté, la vermine Hitler Adolf

même collège, fréquenté à Linz en 1904, c'est écœurante la
mémoire

de nous européens, à tout moment cette ligne de la raison
cette ligne arienne, grecque, romaine, chrétienne, galiléenne
elle déraisonne, elle dérape à nouveau, elle n'arrive pas vraiment
à exister, nous européens c'est dangereux d'être nous-mêmes
de vouloir à tout prix être cette avant-garde de l'humanité
ne soyons pas fidèles à notre mémoire, à nos frontières
si incertaines, nous européens
finalement
ne soyons pas trop nous-mêmes

English translation:

We Europeans

We're doing pretty well
we're not out of our depth
we still have ideas, things to say
we're full of projects, we're very inventive
we're moving things, we're broadening our minds

we Europeans, people hate us

I don't quite get this formula 'We Europeans'
sure I understand the urgency, the requirement of our times
we need to put 'we Europeans' at the beginning
at first it sounds weird, but I'm hooked, by a feeling
of responsibility, 'we Europeans, we aren't
dead yet, we're standing fast, we're here
in good old Europe'
I'd really like to say this, but people can't bear us
we drive them mad
they want to flatten us with lorries, vans, they shoot at us

civilisations are in conflict, and that costs us dear
in surveillance cameras

experienced people, however, say we've done good things
we can be proud, old Europe isn't so old
it modernises all the time, refines itself
we're flexible, there's plenty of tolerance,
we tolerate all that can be tolerated
but it's the people who no longer tolerate us
(me, I would like to become a tolerant European
before being killed by a gas cylinder)

I understand being Italian or French is no longer a big deal
that we must face global competition
with a European moral and political armour
but we must know something about history and geography,
being a good European isn't innate

I hope in any case that if Europe exists
it has a body sufficiently compact and homogeneous
so I can slip inside, a body
without flaws, Judeo-Christian but enlightened
and free-thinking

but we can't always be loved, even our own
hate us, our youngest, they needed
more history and geography, respect
for spelling
we can't be so bad in the end
with all the churches we've built
for centuries nothing but magnificent churches, cathedrals, works
of mercy in stone and marble
and the Hippocratic oath

and our Encyclopaedia
we've always cared about humanity, all of humanity in its entirety
too much sometimes, possibly

but geography above all, good geography courses in school, at college
with the map of Europe spread out on the wall facing us
Europe behind the desk like an abstract, monotonous landscape
coming alive and teeming with mysterious characters as soon as we
approach
as soon as we peer at it: the frail circles of lost villages,
the trembling, fine lines of secondary rivers, the anonymous islands,
pieces
of meaningless land floating far from the coasts, up close this Europe
was going in all directions, we searched for its limits,
a reassuring contour, like the flesh in a firm sausage,
stuffed with peoples and territories, but we never understood
the boundary, on the right, to the east, where did it stop, our common
home?
in Russia or in the Soviet Union? my gaze always sliding over
to the Ural mountains, drawn towards the boundless corridor, the huge
reservoir of space: terrible Siberia, we could stand in the far north
close to the arctic circle, starting at Arkhangelsk, never far from the sea
or alternatively trace a path in the middle, up to the village of Tobolsk
before hitting the edge of the map, there
Siberia disappeared and the classroom wall reappeared, dirty, stupid
without the brilliance of toponymy, and because of that
we never knew where Asia began or Europe ended
and what actually was this great Soviet thing, amorphous
and fascinating, floating in the middle
over there, anyway, the boundary wasn't watertight

the western frontier, though, we were told, held no mysteries:

Spain and Portugal, then the ocean, an all-blue dividing surface
but once again I gravitated towards an upward diagonal
I had a mad longing to go to Reykjavik, far from everywhere, on an
island
where they spoke an improbable language, right at the edge of the map
towards this absolute north no longer with any point of reference
this north that defeated the map-makers' meticulous obstinacy
they hardly drew anything anymore, just simple contours, we didn't
know
if it was sea, land, ice or something else, a different material
but there again the accounts weren't right, we were deprived
by silent amputation, of Greenland, a matter of space-saving
no doubt, but we obscured the tracks again, and I see nothing
here, after cutting up the Kingdom of Denmark, of the 'refinement of
moral feeling', so Renan said, belongs to us, the Indo-Europeans, the
Aryans, where would our proverbial 'sickly grace' be, faced with this
act of butchery
wishing to untangle an unclear western border
to make it easier to put Europe on the map, flat, neat and clean

but Europe isn't just a territory, a matter of borders
or of watersheds, I agree, it's a word and also
a symbolic thing, a profound feeling, a whole history
a billion, I exaggerate, millions of years of culture,
a few hundred at least, we must get into
memory mode: and already I remember Pierre Paul
Rubens, vigour and refinement, there's no one more European
but immediately another comes to mind
six years younger, the rotten Albrecht von Wallenstein
the condottiere, they arise in pairs, the painter-diplomat
and the general-entrepreneur, the height of baroque painting
and the looting and killing machine of the Thirty Years' War

don't get depressed, but if I evoke Ludwig Wittgenstein
the most radical and rambling of philosophers of the last century
he drags that other one with him, the failed painter, the vermin Adolf
Hitler
attended the same Linz college in 1904, it's sickening the memory
we Europeans have, at any time this line of reason
this Aryan, Greek, Roman, Christian, Galilean line
becomes unreasonable, it runs out of control again, it can't really
exist, we Europeans, it's dangerous to be ourselves
to want at all cost to be this vanguard of humanity
to not be true to our memory, to our borders
so uncertain, we Europeans
in the end,
not to be too much ourselves

It's the Law, Stupid

Baroness Helena Kennedy QC

Leaders of the 27 European Union partner countries have now laid down the gauntlet. No discussions on a trade deal will take place until there are positive signs of progress on the border in Ireland and on our commitment to the divorce bill i.e. our contribution to the costs we have incurred on pensions for former UK MEPS and other debts, as well as a contribution to financial projects set in train by the EU while the UK was a signed-up member.

The third 'condition precedent' is that the position of our citizens who live in Europe and those citizens from other European countries who live here has to be secured. We are told there is a document on the table but the UK is not prepared to sign. No reason has been given as to why.

The problem for our Prime Minister is that at every turn her head hits the hard wall of LAW and the role of the European Court of Justice. She has cornered herself, by insisting that the UK withdraws totally from the ECJ and its decisions or 'acquis'. No one had explained to her in advance that if you have cross border rights and contracts, and you want some level of collaboration with Europe, you have to have cross border law and regulations. And if you have cross border law, you have to have supra-national courts to deal with disputes. Even the WTO has a disputes court. You might seek to disguise the fact by calling it by another name but in the end you need rules as to conduct and arbiters for disagreement. But Mrs May has had a bellyful of European courts after her run-in with the totally separate European Court of Human Rights, when she was trying to deport Abu Qatada, the Islamic fundamentalist preacher, to Jordan. Jordan's use of torture on political opponents to secure evidence proved a handicap to his expulsion. However, although all this related to a quite separate legal regime, the words Europe and court in the same sentence invite obstinate opposition from Mrs May.

All the preliminary matters thrown on to the table by the EU leaders involve legal commitments. We have contractual obligations from which we cannot lawfully walk away. Law matters. So all the calls to cut and run without paying a penny in the Brexit settlement are unlawful and unethical. It is not surprising that 'The 27' want to see the colour of our money up front.

Then there is Ireland. The EU feels very involved with the Irish border question. The EU role in the peace negotiations should not be underestimated; much EU time and resource has gone into securing an end to the violence. Ireland's sectarian divide became submerged in an overarching European identity, which made it possible for Ireland to function with no visible border. Indeed, the Irish dairy industry is likely to be devastated by any return to a hard border because dairy herds are located north and south and the 'shopfloor' spreads across the invisible line. The same is true of many other businesses and social ventures. The communal life throughout Ireland has been deepened by the peace agreement. There is a real risk that any new border or customs posts would be to be blown-up in short order and the full horrors of the past could return; angry Republican nationalists are feeling deeply affronted that in the interests of securing peace, the South of Ireland amended its Constitutional claim of right to the seven counties of the North, only to have the carpet pulled from under them by the UK leaving the EU.

Increasingly, there is talk that the only possible way to preserve a soft border in Ireland is for a special deal to be negotiated for Northern Ireland, whatever the rest of the UK does, by possibly joining the European Economic Area with some additional border arrangements between the North and the UK to prevent Ireland being a backdoor into the UK. None of this is easy and many Unionists will be outraged if the border becomes one between Northern Ireland and the UK mainland and, as they are saying in Ireland, squaring this circle will take God's own patience and ingenuity.

The EEA is a semi-detached position that Norway, Iceland and Lichtenstein have signed up to, whereby they have the benefits of the single market but not the full commitments. However, it also has legal implications. You cannot trade without the protection of law because things can go wrong. The EEA members have to sign up to EFTA, the European Free Trade Association, a special supranational judicial body or court which deals with disputes; it sits in Luxembourg, and is run largely according to EU law and ECJ judgements. Of course, such law is made without the input of EEA states, which makes it a solution that would be hard for many Brexiteers to swallow.

In preparation for the negotiations, the countries which belong to the EU delegations have been streaming through the Lords and Commons Committees and meeting with Brexit ministers. They are invariably bemused. They say that they keep being told that the UK wants to continue to be part of the European Arrest Warrant, Europol and Eurojust (for police and courts to collaborate on international crime, terrorism and trafficking) yet don't seem to understand that this requires the ECJ to have ultimate jurisdiction and for EU law to apply. It seems obvious to them that cross border collaboration requires supra-national legal arrangements.

They list all the vast areas of law covering the web of relationships that exist from financial services, to trading, to farming, to fishing, to security, to environment, to employment, to maternity rights, to trading standards and consumer rights. Intellectual Property Law, for example, covers a huge array of research, entrepreneurship, invention and creativity; the European Patent Court has only recently been built here in London and was due to be opened. What happens to it now, they ask?

For years the British public have been subjected to a barrage of tabloid mendacity, suggesting we are victims of an onslaught of foreign invented law and interference by foreign courts. In fact, vast amounts of incredibly advantageous law has been created in the EU in the last 40 years and, here is the rub, WE have been major contributors to that law. The British are good at law. We have had a strong hand in its creation.

The Committee which I chair in the House of Lords has heard overwhelming evidence about the benefits to British business of being able to take a contractual matter to one of our own courts, secure a judgment against a recalcitrant debtor in Poland or somewhere, and the judgment will be enforced in a court in that part of the EU without demur. A mother of children can secure a maintenance order against their renegade father, who has sloped off to Italy, and have the order enforced in Milan. A British father can get access to his kids ordered in Munich. Cross border relationships require cross border law, and agreements on mutual enforcement are fundamental. A holiday accident in Spain or Portugal can lead to swifter resolution and compensation by virtue of EU law.

No wonder it is suggested that Theresa May seems to be on

another galaxy with her imagining that she can have the best of Europe without its institutions or legal underpinnings. Her fantasy that the Great Repeal Act will fix the problem by bringing all this law home or that a deal can be done without the need for any European court is unravelling. These legal arrangements require reciprocity. The courts of EU countries do things for us because we do likewise for them. A piece of unilateral legislation on our part does not secure that mutuality which is embodied in many regulations.

Harmonising law across Europe has raised standards – to our advantage. Europe-wide law is now integrated into our lives, albeit without much visibility, but it makes our European engagement safer and stronger. In the 'new order' of new deals with China and others none of these safeguards will exist. My guess is that if Mrs May does secure a deal with the EU, we will find ourselves quietly signing up to a newly created court or tribunal, a lesser ECJ.

The law, judges and courts are all being attacked by the 'Hard Right' now in many democracies, from Mr Trump's assaults in the USA to those in Poland, Hungary and Turkey. It is the currency of our dangerous times. Deregulation means attacking the very law and rules, which actually protect ordinary people from the raw transactions of hyper-marketisation. Be warned. Good law is a protection we have to preserve. The price of its loss will be very high indeed.

[Part of this article was first published in The Guardian, 3 May 2017.]

Health Care and Brexit: a View from the Cliff Edge

Jean McHale

The NHS provided the backdrop to the referendum with the pledge on the side of the big red bus of £350 million a week to the NHS. Nonetheless, as the dust has settled it is increasingly apparent that Brexit will have consequences for the NHS other than a simple transfer of cash to provide enhanced services. Critically, Brexit will impact on people – on patients and on health professionals. Currently individuals have a range of rights consequent upon EU membership. Use of the European Health Insurance Card (EHIC) gives a UK citizen in another EEA country access to free or subsidised emergency health care. The EU Regulation 883/2004 through what is known as the S1 Scheme enables UK citizens who are retirees in another member state to have the cost of their medical treatment reimbursed. On Brexit D-Day if these issues are not resolved, UK citizens receiving treatment in other member states could suddenly find that they are asked to pay unexpected bills for their care, confronted with a credit card machine and the words 'Visa, American Express or Mastercard?'. The latest information from the negotiations suggests that some agreements may be possible on these issues but we are unclear as to which patients and when. Existing citizens' rights will hopefully be safeguarded, but the longer term position remains uncertain on such things as the EHIC card. The government has indicated that there may be some form of the EHIC card for UK citizens in the future – but it is very unclear as to exactly how this will work. Unless the EU is prepared to operate a scheme as at present UK citizens may be faced with paying for emergency treatment up front and then subsequently trying to claim reimbursement when they return – assuming they have the necessary money to pay upfront for expensive medical care. Without reciprocal rights UK citizens will need to ensure as with the United States that when they travel they have fully comprehensive health insurance. Other rights too are in question – the EU Patients' Rights Directive gives patients some rights to obtain treatment in another EU member state e.g. where they have suffered undue delay through waiting lists – these rights very are likely to cease post Brexit.

The precise nature of health law rights has another dimension in relation to cross-border care between Northern Ireland and the Republic of Ireland. For many years there has been co-operation in health care provision and patients are sent across the border for treatment. Any return to a hard border could have very serious consequences indeed for patient care, not simply in relation to long term planned care but also emergency treatment. Professional mobility is a further issue – there are real concerns that Brexit may have adverse effects on NHS staffing. Estimates suggest that some 5% overall of the NHS workforce is drawn from other EU member states but in some parts of the country in particular London that number is much higher. At a time when there are existing staff shortages the NHS can ill afford to lose the services of highly skilled health professionals. Securing their position in the Brexit negotiations is also critical.

The EU has also impacted on a raft of issues which affect patient safety. So for example, EU Directives regulate the quality and safety of blood (a matter of current controversy in the light of compensation for those who have suffered in the past as a result of transfusions of contaminated blood), of tissues and of organs. Some of this legislation may be incorporated under the EU With-drawal Bill provisions into UK law but what happens in the future in relation to health care standards – will we align ourselves with EU and other international standards in relation to quality and safety in the future or will we fall by the wayside? Take another issue – the privacy of our own personal health information. EU data protection law is important not simply in terms of patient access to their own information but in relation to the use of patient information in the NHS and in clinical research. The government is introducing new legislation to align UK law with a new EU Data Protection Regulation which is due to be passed pre-Brexit but while this may alleviate concerns for the short term, long term questions remain as to what Brexit will mean for patient data and its usage.

Pharmaceutical regulation and clinical research involving medi-cinal products is yet another area where our regulation is indebted to the EU. When we leave the EU and acquire third country status we may simply be regarded as a 'second priority launch market' by pharmaceutical companies. In relation to clinical drug trials this area is currently governed by an EU Directive due to be replaced in 2019 by a new EU regulation. It appears that this is due to be implemented after we leave the EU – so do we decide to comply with it or not? On the one hand, it may be seen as a good approach to take, not least to facilitate participation in cross-border clinical trials but in practice it is not quite so simple. There are advantages in terms of being able to carry out trials in several states and to better market the drug – but there will also be costs. Or do we want to pick and choose aspects of it? The Regulation involves degrees of reciprocity including participation in a new computer portal which will operate across the EU – will we be allowed to have access to this by our EU cousins? Medicinal products regulation involves reciprocity in other ways such as databases enabling serious adverse reactions to drugs to be made available to other member states; without special provisions in the negotiations we will be cut out of these post Brexit. Again the safety of medical devices including in vitro devices is all currently subject to EU Directives; a new system will need to be put in place to address these questions if an effective agreement is not reached as part of the negotiations.

These are just a few of the challenges ahead. EU law has helped us start to frame at least some of the regulation of health care in this country – to shape a UK patient as an EU patient – the question remains: how much if any of this will in a decade's time remain? The EU Withdrawal Bill is working its way through Parliament yet at the time of writing in October 2017, almost six months since Article 50 was triggered, there are still very many issues which remain unclear and that the government is still a long way from truly engaging with – in public at least – at the level of granular detail which will be needed to properly inform the Brexit negotiating process. The clock is ticking – March 2019 is looming, a transitional deal may be implemented of course. That would at least provide a degree of breathing space – but it can only be viewed as that. The clock will still be ticking in such a situation – even though the deadline is extended somewhat. In relation to health care as with other areas these negotiations are truly important in shaping the nature and delivery of many areas of the NHS in the future. As we lurch towards the cliff-edge it is clear that without an effective Brexit settlement we risk damaging the health of the nation.

Fall Out

Petra McQueen

The morning after Brexit, Sophie threw her clothes into the pull-along suitcase they'd bought for their honeymoon and sat on it, wrenching the zip with a strangled shout, 'You're a fascist.'

He folded his arms and leaned against the door frame to stop himself from shaking her self-righteous head off her shoulders. 'At least I'm not a libtard loser.'

'What even,' she stood from the suitcase, red-faced and sweaty, 'does that mean?'

He pursed his lips.

She pushed past him and onto the landing. 'You don't know, do you?' She pulled the suitcase behind her on the stairs. It thumped on each one. 'You sit there on the Internet laughing at all those stupid men's jokes, and you don't get it.' She wrenched open the front door. 'What about our kids' future?'

'We don't have any.'

'I know!' She slammed the door so hard that the house shook.

He ran to the bedroom window, flung it open. 'I'm not a fascist.'

Some men, putting up bunting for the village fete, looked up, but Sophie continued her march.

'My granddad fought in the war!'

She turned, one hand on the trolley, feet square as though she'd punch him if close enough. 'I wish he'd been shot,' she shouted, 'then you wouldn't be here.'

A burst of laughter from the workmen. 'You tell him, love!'

Jake slammed the window shut. The bedroom was a mess: unmade bed, strewn clothes, wardrobe and drawers gaping like she'd robbed the place. A spill of brown puddled on the cream rug where he'd flung the duvet back so quickly that it had caught his mug on the bedside table and brought it tumbling. Both of them had been too angry to care. He closed the door on the mess and went down to the front room, drawing the curtains against workmen directing lorries onto the Green. As he sat at the computer, he could hear a bloke with a mega-phone, the words so distorted that Jake wasn't sure if he was shouting 'Stand clear' or 'All clear.'

He turned the sound as loud as it would go and played Grand Theft Auto. For a few short moments in each game, the violence of the guns swept him up, but mostly thoughts of Sophie buzzed. So what if her side had lost? Weren't the results from yesterday her great democracy in action? When they'd wrangled over the issues in the past few months: her pressing for actual European laws he despised, him standing up for Great Britain, he'd seen it as a kind of game. He was Bubba, in Liberty City, finding the next telephone box. Sophie was the cops, dead-end streets, even the rules of the game itself. He didn't think he'd actually complete the mission. He'd no idea he'd get to the finish and find himself victorious but without the game to play anymore.

Unable to distract himself from his bursting bladder any longer, he went to the loo. As he pissed a gushing stream, he looked out of the window. The group of hi-vis wankers were cordoning off the Green with twisted metal bars and ticker-tape. Lorries belched out fumes and a stage was being set up.

With a sudden lurch, he remembered that Sophie had invited a few of their mates over for drinks the next day, preloading before the fete began. He put down the loo seat and sat on it. On his phone, he found the group message and wrote: *Soz everyone. Can't do drinks at*

He hesitated, about to write *ours*, when the full force of Sophie leaving hit him. He wept sobs so loud that they echoed along the tiles. The noise shocked him but he couldn't stop. They'd only been married five months but they'd been seeing each other for three years. Why would she throw all that away on something so stupid? Why was she such a stubborn stuck-up cow? Hadn't he done everything for her? Worked night shifts in the clamour of the Ford Factory, an hour's commute away, just so she could do her social work training? That was her problem: six months at the university and she'd turned into one of *them*. Even her clothes had got frumpy.

He wiped his eyes and dialled her number. A few short rings and her voice mail switched on. Stupid cow was screening her calls. 'You need to come over straight away and pick up the rest of your stuff,' he said. 'And *you* can cancel tomorrow not me.' He rang off and flung his phone, wincing as it clattered on the tiles. He scuttled and picked it up. A fine crack across the screen scarred Sophie's face.

A message flashed up. *U alrite m8.* Even before he'd read the name, he knew, by the way it was written, that it was from Tommy, his best mate.

Yeah why?

Msg from S

So she'd got his voice mail and already told everyone rather than ring up and apologise. The phone beeped again. *What haps, m8*

Jake closed his eyes and took a deep breath. The phone rang and Micky the Meat's face appeared on the screen. Here they came, like vultures, wanting to pick open his wounds. It was showing Sophie Big Al's meme of the Queen giving two fingers to Merkel that had started the row in the first place.

The ringing stopped and another message from Tommy popped up. *Fuck Sophie get pissed with me and boys tmrw at fete.* Jake's fingers hovered over the screen, then he wrote, *Sure meet you there.* The glass was rough at the crack.

At work, in the long hours of the night shift, his phone remained silent. He kept it in his pocket, expecting it to buzz, checking every few minutes in case there was a message from Sophie. He didn't like her right now, didn't see why she'd fallen on the side of the snowflakes, but she was his wife. He still loved her, didn't he?

The question niggled inside him as some Polski asked him about his rights to stay at the company: 'As foreman you must have information.'

'None of us know, mate,' he said, glad when the siren rang and drowned out the man's voice, giving him an excuse to escape. He drove home in the yellow light of dawn and wondered if it was too early to knock Sophie up at her sister's where she must be staying. No, he was damned if he'd beg her to come back. She needed to be the one to make the first move. She owed him that.

The loudspeaker from the Green woke him: a bass cacophony of distorted words. He lay, stoned with sleep for a second or two, then remembered how Sophie had up and left. Without even brushing his teeth, he flung on his clothes and went to the fete.

He walked past the stage, where a group of primary school kids shuffled into lines, and onto the large Green. To his right was the beer tent and fast food vans. On the other side, stalls: Hook-a-

Duck, Tombola, Home-made cakes, that sort of thing. A make-shift fun fair sat at the end, with a bouncy castle, a Merry-Go-Round and an old fashioned Big Wheel, gleaming in the mid-morning sun.

The Green was packed and Jake was momentarily confused by the outfits: middle-aged women got up as serving wenches, old guys in soldiers' uniforms, kids as Victorian urchins, until he remembered that this year it was fancy dress. He didn't think there'd been a theme, but it seemed as though everyone had decided to come as something from Ye Olde England. Makes you proud, he thought, but the words sounded half-hearted in his head.

He strode to the beer tent.

'Aye, aye!' Tommy shouted over from a table. Micky the Meat and Big Al were with him. All of them wore union Jack T-shirts and kiss-me-quick hats.

Jake spread out his arms. 'Looking good, boys!'

They lifted up their pints, gave him a roar of approval. Tommy tossed him a hat. 'Got you one too, mate.'

Jake picked it up and pulled a face. 'Kiss-me-Quick?'

Tommy clapped him on the shoulder. 'You might need it now.'

Jake felt his lips go tight. He put the hat on the table. 'I'll just get meself a pint.'

As he walked away, he heard Micky the Meat say, 'You're such a dick, Tommy,' and Tommy's reply, 'Come off it: he's better off without her.'

He stood in line at the bar behind a Town Crier and tried not to think. The marquee smelt of trapped summer air and spilled ale. 'What do you want?' said a girl, with a scooped blouse and a high bodice from which her tits rose like two white bloomers. 'Old Peculier, Aspalls, or Carlsberg?'

Once upon a time he would've flirted with her, but he'd lost the knack. Maybe Tommy was right, and he'd need it again. His heart sank, but he tried a smile and a small wink. 'Carlsberg, sweetheart.'

'Hi, Jake!'

He looked up to see Sandra, Sophie's boss when she'd worked at The Bulldog, waving at him from another pump. From her bright smile, he could tell the news hadn't reached her yet. 'You looking for Soph?' she said, placing a pint in front of a man dressed as a nun. 'She's not on this shift, she's over at the burger van.'

Sophie was here? Helping out? Had she arranged it before she'd left or put her name down at the last minute? Did she want to 'accidentally' bump into him? His fingers shook as he lifted up his pint and took a long drink. He looked at the white bubbles smearing the plastic and ordered another. Sod her. If she wanted to find him, she could guess well enough where he'd be.

He walked back to the table, a pint in each hand. The men were deep in discussion about Brexit. 'Best thing to have happened to our country,' said Big Al. 'All that money we send there, we can use on our people, the people that matter.'

Micky the Meat wiped his mouth. 'What I hate is when people call me racist. This isn't about race. You should see the amount of forms we have to fill in just to sell a slab of bacon.'

The men shook their heads in sympathy. 'That's what all those nobs don't get,' said Tommy. 'They're not dealing with the day to day shit. They're just happy little Arabella can get a grant to ballet dance in Lichtenstein.'

'That's not part of the EU,' said Jake. It had come up with Sophie for some reason and she'd called him an idiot. Her! The girl who was nothing more than a jumped-up barmaid, now covered up to her arms in grease at the burger van.

'Fucking Zurich, then,' said Tommy. 'You get what I mean.'

They each took a long drink. 'So,' said Micky the Meat, leaning towards Jake, 'you all right with... you know?'

'Course he is,' said Tommy.

'Not talking to you. Mates should be able to speak about what matters.'

'You been reading your girl's Cosmo again?' said Big Al.

Micky the Meat rolled his eyes. 'You two aren't married. You don't get it. Something like that can change a man. Might think you hate them, that they get on your tits, and you're better off without. But it's the small things you miss. When my Heather upped sticks, I was glad for about a week, but then I...' He trailed off, picked up his pint and took a long drink.

Tommy and Big Al raised their eyebrows at each other, but Jake found himself inching forward.

Micky the Meat gave him a sad smile and wrinkled his nose. 'Not having the kids around was the worst of it. But it was the small things too. Someone to chat to about nothing, the house a damn sight cleaner than it is now, the money too... Didn't think her little wage would account for much but it did.' He touched Jake's arm. 'All I'm saying, mate, is if there's any chance of making it up, you should give it a go.'

'Don't know about that,' said Tommy.

The three men turned to him and he squirmed in his seat. 'I'm not being mean or nothing but your Sophie can be a right royal pain in the arse.'

That was his wife! Jake bunched his hands into fists and held them under the table.

'Remember that time she kicked me out for saying Paki Shop?' Big Al laughed.

'That's what I calls it, don't mean anything by it.'

'It wasn't just that though,' said Jake, through gritted teeth. 'You were properly pissed, and you called her a mong.'

'Well, she shouldn't have had a go. Mardy-cow.'

Big Al put his hand on Tommy's wrist. Tommy looked down at it and gave a sigh. He tilted his chin to Jake. 'Soz, mate.'

Was he? Tommy had been funny with him ever since Sophie and he had started getting serious, banging on about how Jake was boring now. He couldn't see he'd changed that much, he was still the same old Jake, one of the lads. Course, he never made it to darts nights anymore, but that was because of the night shifts. With a little jump, he realised that if Sophie had gone, he wouldn't have to do nights anymore, could get a lodger to help with the rent. He buried the idea. Of course, he wanted Sophie back.

Jake swept his eyes along the table, chocka with empty glasses. He needed to catch up. 'Pint anyone?'

'That's more like it,' said Tommy.

As he made his way to the bar, he saw Sophie through the flap of the tent. The shock of her stopped him in his tracks long enough to register what she wore: a skirt of England flags, a white t-shirt and a blue silk scarf tied around her neck. As gorgeous as ever, the skirt flapped up over her long, tanned legs. He ran after her and tapped her on the shoulder.

She turned with a smile which fell. 'Oh, it's you.'

Now he saw that the scarf had little yellow stars on it. He took a step back. 'Why did you marry me?'

'Not now, Jake.' She turned and walked away.

She wore red high heels, so it was easy to catch up with her. He marched by her side. 'When then? When can we talk? You can't just leave me.'

She faced him, arms folded. 'Why not?'

'We're married.' He felt shameful tears rise. 'You knew what I was like the day we got hitched.'

She flushed and looked at the ground. By her feet was a crumpled can of Stella.

He leaned forward. 'Didn't you?'

'I thought... I thought it didn't matter.' She tilted her chin and swallowed. 'I told myself I wanted to be with you forever, have kids but –'

He caught hold of her hand. 'Is that it? I know I said I wasn't keen, but if that's what–'

She twisted her hand away. 'No, Jake. Not with you.' She walked quickly, slamming her heels into the ground. A dog ran past Jake, followed by a hollering group of Scouts, blocking his path. A few strides later he almost tripped over a mobility scooter ridden by St. George.

When he caught up with her, Sophie was standing in the queue for the Big Wheel.

He stood next to her, panting. 'What are you doing?'

'What does it look like?' Her voice was brittle. 'Can't I have a bit of fun on my break?'

He looked at the wheel, the flaking carny-painted seats, and decided not to point out it looked like a pile of shit. 'Can't we talk instead?'

She gave a quick shake of her head, but from the way she stood so still, he knew she'd listen. 'This Brexit thing,' he said, 'it's not like it's life or death. What has any of it got to do with us?'

'I... I didn't leave you because I'm a sore loser. It just, I think, it helped me see...'

'See what?'

She studied the floor and mumbled, 'What you're really like.'

'What am I like?' He lifted up his hands. 'I'm just me.'

Her face softened as she looked at him. 'I wish... I wish you'd see the world like I do. It's not like you think it is. There's not an us and a them. It's just one family.'

He tried hard not to roll his eyes, but she caught his expression. 'This is never going to work. We're too different.'

She moved forward in the queue and he had to step with her to hear her voice over the music. '...when I gave that beggar a tenner?' she was saying. 'Or when I wanted to pick up all the rubbish that time in Crete?'

He couldn't even recall the moment she was talking about, saw only the white of her bikini on the golden sand.

'Or when I told you about Shanine's benefits being cut and you said she was a scrounger? She's got two kids on her own.'

Another thing he'd forgotten. She must have been storing this up for weeks, hating him all this time. He didn't need to put up with this: her resentment, that confidence that everything she believed in was right and he was nothing but that black picture she'd painted.

'You two lovebirds next,' said the man at the gate.

Jake stepped back.

'You coming, mate?' said the man.

Sophie opened out her hands as if to say it was his choice, that they could talk some more if he wanted. He shook his head wanting nothing more to do with her. Chin down, she sat on the seat and pulled the bar down. As the wheel creaked into action she wouldn't look at him. He didn't want her to.

Jake walked back towards the Beer tent and as he moved closer, he could hear 'Jerusalem' belted out by a group of drunks inside. The last time he'd sung it was at his wedding.

He turned. Sophie was travelling to the top of the circle. It must have been cold up there as she'd unknotted her scarf and laid it flat across her shoulders. The blue background and small yellow stars flapped against the side of the carriage. Jake imagined himself sitting next to her, the soft silky feel of the scarf, her warm body, red roofs, green fields, and the lake he'd fished in as a boy. Should he go to her, take the next trip round?

His chest moved forwards as though about to run to her, but his feet stayed where they were, planted on the grass, stubborn and heavy, as though he could no longer move forward or back.

Because I Could (or What the EU Did for Me)

Giacinto Palmieri

The EU means different things to different people. To some, it means the mythical 'unaccountable Brussels bureaucrats'; to others, the equally mythical banana curvature normalising over-regulation. Something abstract, remote. To me, instead, the EU is something that has had a very concrete impact on my life: freedom of movement. More specifically, being egocentric as I am, the EU is *my* freedom of movement. I'll tell you why.

I was never good at remembering dates and anniversaries, not even mine, but for some reason this one has remained firmly impressed on my memory: 5 March 2001. It is the date when, from my native Milan, I moved to London. I was asked many times *why* I made that choice and I always found it difficult to reply. Truth is, I didn't have any of the classic 'hard' reasons: I wasn't sent abroad by my company, I wasn't unemployed in Italy (actually, I had a very well paid IT consulting job), I didn't have to re-join a family. What happened, instead, is that I had just come out of both a long personal relationship and a business partnership. Moreover, I had attended a course on some software product in Slough (yes,

not even that put me off England) and realised, with some surprise, that my English would be good enough for me to work in
England. In other words, the best way in which I can explain my
choice of moving to London is by quoting an old dirty joke: 'Do
you know why dogs lick their own genitals? Because they can.'

I had sent some CVs from Italy before my arrival, so I arrived
on a Monday, had my first interview with a company on the same
day, got a second interview for the Wednesday and received a
very good job offer on the Friday of the same week (this was
before the financial crisis). Nothing in my experience in Italy had
ever been so quick or so easy! I'll never forget the buzz I felt: I
had taken what, back then, I perceived as a big risk, moving to a
place where I didn't know anybody, without a job and with only
a sketchy knowledge of the language... and the gamble had paid
off! In Italy (particularly in the South, where my parents and all
my relatives are from), you are educated to think that you always
need to 'know somebody' if you want to get anything in life. In the
following years, I was reminded of this shared belief many times,
when relatives, distant relatives, very distant relatives, friends of
very distant relatives and, sometimes, friends of friends of very
distant relatives thought that the person they *knew* in London, and
who would help them to find a job or a room, was nobody else but
me. Regularly, I explained to them how I had found my job and my
accommodation without knowing anybody, directing them to the
same websites and agencies I had used and offering advice on how
to adapt their CV to London's job market. What I *really* meant to
say was: the beauty of London is that here you don't *need* to know
anybody, don't spoil it, don't bring the bad habits and insecurities
back with you from the old country! And that is the reason why
there are parts of Italy where I'm no longer welcome.

I'm not saying that there were no aspects of British life which I
found challenging or puzzling. On the contrary. The way I reacted

to the puzzlement was by trying to put it into words. This is the first piece I ever wrote in English and I'll quote it in full, it being very short. Yes, I know, that's very self-referential. Indeed, it is often said that I'm too self-referential... by me, mostly. In any case, here it is. As you will see, it is a mock ethnographic study:

Among the natives of the island of Britain, the ceremony known as 'Office Christmas Party' plays an important social role. The most colourful and elaborate costumes are worn, according to a complex code of symbols. Some participants, for example, dress as prominent figures of the community, such as the policeman or the fireman. Asked about the meaning of their costumes, the natives reportedly say that they were impersonating the 'village people'. Unfortunately, little is known about what really happens during the party. This is probably due to some code of secrecy, or at least this is the most believable theory to explain why, when interviewed the following morning, most people declared that they couldn't remember a thing. According to some reports, however, an important part seems to be constituted by the rite known as 'photocopying the bum'. Images produced during this rite are currently under the scrupulous scrutiny of the experts. Along with the natives, non-native members of the community are also reported to take part in these ceremonies. In relation to their social rank, they are known to the natives as 'foreign residents', 'economic immigrants' or 'bloody asylum seekers'. During the Christmas Party, they are easily recognisable by their air of confusion and for the mixed results of their attempts to blend in. In a particularly gruesome episode, an unfortunate non-native is believed to have mistaken the shredder for the photocopier.

I intended to send this piece to a friend of mine called Adrian, but by mistake I sent it to the MD of my company, also called Adrian. Instead of firing me, he read it in front of everybody during the *actual* office Christmas party! Making people laugh. He didn't mention my name, thinking he should protect the identity of an innocent, but I thought he should have: he was getting *my* laughs! On the other hand, it gave me the impression that in this new country I couldn't do anything wrong, not even by mistake. A few days later, I was in a pub by myself (as I prefer to say, instead of 'alone') when I noticed a sign advertising a comedy night. I went in and it was a revelation: here is where I could get *my* laughs! My new country kept giving me new ideas and offering new opportunities, and that, still, without the need to know anybody. All I needed to know, even better, all I needed *not* to know, was what I was doing.

So, I started doing stand-up comedy. There are three types of stand-up comedians: natural writers who need to learn how to perform, natural performers who need to learn how to write and the lucky bastards. It soon became clear that I belonged to the first category (yes, I know, calling myself a natural writer while at the same time exposing my writing to your kind but undoubtedly discerning and unforgiving judgement, is very hubristic of me, but this entire piece is hubristic, if not the entire moving-to-London experience this piece is about, so please put up with it). I joined a course to gain some stage confidence, I did my first gig and I was hooked. I improved my performing skills enough to gain a place on (but not a placement in) the final of the Hackney Empire New Act of the Year 2010 competition. I remember opening with the following routine:

As an Italian I have always been suspicious of social networks. For instance: the Mafia. Yes, it is a social network, it's a network of friends of friends, I think they should use Facebook. It would go something like this: 'Jackie the Nose has sent you an offer of friendship you can't refuse. Please deny any knowledge of him. Your friend Al the Animal has written a message on the Wall. Grassing you up. Please click here to change his profile.

Your friend Al the Animal has poked your eyes out.' They should call it ScarFacebook. Great, I'm Italian, I have done the Mafia jokes, I can move on now.

I'm not sure it really worked, though, given that a reviewer commented: 'The audience took a while to warm to Giacinto Palmieri, perhaps trying to work out if his very thick Italian accent meant he was a character act.' Yes, my accent was too thick for me to sound believable! With reviews like this, who needs to write jokes? I got a bigger response with the following joke:

'You do this and that and Bob's your uncle.' That's a strange expression, what does it mean? I did a bit of research: apparently, there was a Prime Minister in Victorian times, Robert Cecil, nicknamed Bob, who was very nepotistic, so people started to say: 'everything is easy when Bob is your uncle.' I think there should be an Italian equivalent. It would go: 'you do this and that and Silvio fucked your daughter.'

Yes, Silvio Berlusconi and his antics. What a gold mine he was (*is*) for comedians! Mentioning his name sometimes was enough to get a laugh. In any case, performing at the beautiful Hackney Empire was an amazing, Cinderella-like experience (in the sense that afterwards I went back to performing in the function rooms of pubs). Little did I know that it was going to be the last year that the competition was to be performed there. That sort of reverse Midas-touch was going to be a constant of my experience in London. In other words, if my new country was good for me, I wasn't sure I was good for it: my favourite print newspaper was *The Independent* (do you remember it?), my mortgage provider was Northern Rock (do you remember it?), my favourite bookshop was Borders (do you remember it?), my football team was West Ham United (do you remember them?), my political party of choice the Lib Dems (and do you remember them?). Ok, the last two are still around, but they did almost disappear in the lower divisions of sport and politics in the years after I started following them. Once, during a holiday in Italy, I heard the Turkish-born, Rome-based film director Ferzan Özpetek speaking at some event: his talk was full of nostalgia for the lost Rome he had originally moved to. I was enraged: if you choose a new place, I thought, you should also accept its ability and freedom to change! But, maybe, it's inevitable for us immigrants to get stuck on the image of our new country exactly as it was when we moved, hoping it would never change. On other hand, we shouldn't publicise this supposed reverse Midas-touch too much, if we don't want to give ammunition to those who think that immigrants are bad for the host country. Yet, since I left Milan, the city has gone through a new Renaissance... yes, correlation does not entail causation... but let's talk of something else.

So, after six years in Britain, I decided to become a British citizen (which, you might argue, is another instance of the reverse Midas-touch... oops). Back then, nobody could understand why a EU citizen might want to become British, given that we enjoyed (most of) the same rights anyway. Maybe I was like a suicidal rat: I couldn't ignore a sinking ship. In any case, I passed the 'Life in the UK' test, with its silly question about what you are supposed to do if you spill somebody's drink (buy another one) or about Father Christmas being 'a cheerful old man with a white beard and a red suit' (were the authorities worried that sightings of Osama Bin Laden might be left unreported by mistake?). I even agreed to swear my loyalty to the Queen and, even more worryingly, to her heirs and successors: I asked if I could at least skip a generation, but sadly I was denied that opportunity. However, behind the stand-up comedian's almost mandatory mask of cynicism, there was also, for the first time in my life, a real desire to belong. Apparently, I spent the first part of my life trying *not* to belong to things I was naturally supposed to belong to and the second part of it trying to belong to things nobody expected me to. For instance, when in Italy I always considered supporting a football team as something too tribal for my liking. Once I moved to the East End of London, however, I found myself supporting the Hammers (yes, that community of supporters so well known for their acceptance of outsiders, foreigners and minorities), mostly because their song *Forever blowing bubbles* reminded me of my relationship with women ('fortune is always hiding / I've looked everywhere / I'm forever blowing bubbles / pretty bubbles in the air'). More generally, I discovered that I'm not against belonging as such, it's just that I want to *choose* what I belong to, instead of having it imposed on me by the postcode lottery of birthplace.

The only, great disappointment of my relationship with Britain was the Brexit vote. My status as a British citizen means that I don't need to worry about the right to stay, but that just makes me feel as if I have found myself a place on Schindler's list. In other words, I suffer from survivor's guilt. New citizens should have the opportunity of composing a Schindler's list of their own, of friends or family who they want to 'save' along with themselves. That way, at least something good would come out of this sorry story: my UK-based EU friends would treat me well. As it is, I can't see any redeeming feature about Brexit. I still hope that it will never happen and that we can keep moving to the UK from (the rest of) the EU – and, equally importantly, the other way round – for the best of all reasons: because we can.

Future in the Cards

Robert Ronsson

In another country that was 1960, when I was ten years old, kids were filthy and feral. Every weekday morning, I left the house after a superficial wipe with a cold flannel across my face, hands and bare knees. Tidemarks showed where the recently cleaned parts merged with the grubby whole. We bathed infrequently – not many houses in our area had bathrooms with running hot water – and we scrabbled in filth and dust, on the way to school, in the playground, on the fringes of the greenbelt and in the traffic-free streets. We had short breaks to refuel and stopped only when it was too dark to see a ball. At the end of the day, we endured another wipe down before bed. With clothes being changed only once a week, teachers must have had strong stomachs to enter wet-Friday classrooms full of steaming boys.

Play rather than family, gave focus and structure to our lives and school lessons were tolerated as the necessary interludes between playtimes ruled over by two swaggering all-boy gangs. The word 'gangs' makes them sound more dangerous than they were. They had more in common with 'The Outlaws' of Richmal Crompton's *Just William* books than the knife carrying, territory-defending street gangs of recent times.

We were no more than gatherings of raggedy-arsed boys with similar natures and interests who looked after each other. The worst you could expect from a rival gang, if they picked on you while you were isolated from your friends, was a 'scragging' that involved teasing and name-calling, and the occasional ineffectual one-to-one 'bundle' – a roll around the floor in which neither combatant inflicted any real blows. Perhaps we were infected with our parents' so recent memories of the war and real violence wasn't in our genes.

The gang leaders in our playground were David Rowe and Richard Ecland. The Rowe gang came from the council estate that bordered three sides of the school and was more aggressive. They spent their happiest moments messing up other kids' games and picking on outsiders. We Eclands, who lived in the terrace facing the school entrance, came together as a defence mechanism. There was protection in numbers.

When we weren't playing football, the Eclands focused on our twin obsessions: bus spotting and football cards. Every boy growing up in the London suburbs was likely to be a bus spotter. You carried your *Ian Allan Guide* that listed all the bus types and bus numbers in the London Transport fleet. When you saw a new one, you crossed off its number in the book. Our gang had the convention that the eyes of one were the eyes of all. This meant that, if one of the gang went up to the City or out into the countryside and came back with numbers of buses that never came to our neighbourhood, we'd all count them as seen. My older brother said this was cheating but he was never in a gang.

The gang rules also governed the trading of football cards. The *Topps Bubble Gum* company gave away a card with each stick of gum. They were team photos of the 22 football clubs in the first division and head-and-shoulder portraits of the leading three or four players in each team. It meant there were about 100 cards in total to collect. Our rule was that we could only trade cards within the gang and, although one of us might unwrap a card that was rarer and worth two or more 'swapsies' in the playground, we could only trade internally one-for-one.

Richard Ecland appreciated that we needed to trade outside the gang to get fresh cards into our closed market and he arranged the external swaps. When an outsider came to him for trade, the gang would pool our swapsies, thus strengthening his negotiating position. As the school year went on we recruited new members to our original nine and they brought in fresh cards. I worried, though, that the new kids were changing the gang's nature and weakening my influence over its decision-making.

Everything changed the day Christopher Allan, who wasn't in either gang, came into the playground offering everybody free bubble gum. His family was posh – it was rumoured that his dad was *the* Ian Allen who published the bus-spotting guides – and he'd been given enough money to buy a whole box of bubble gums. In one go he had 144 cards! This is a time when most of us received only enough pocket money for two or three cards a week. Not only did he stand a good chance of picking up the rarer cards but he had loads of swapsies to trade.

Some of the other Ecland kids, especially the new ones, started doing trades direct with Christopher Allan. It made me disillusioned with the restrictions of the gang and I wanted the freedom to do the same; I wanted to get back control. I told Richard I was leaving.

On the first day of free trading, I unwrapped a new gum and, with my blood fizzing, discovered a rare card that I already had but wasn't in general circulation. It was the Chelsea team card and I knew who to go to with this valuable new swapsie. I sauntered across the playground to the coal bunkers where Phillip Washington was, as usual, perched on one of its black-powdered ledges. He was a big kid, big enough to have existed outside of a gang; he'd always been a loner. I knew he was a Chelsea supporter.

'You got the Chelsea team card yet?' I asked.

He shook his head.

I flourished my swapsies, fanning them out with the Chelsea card on top. 'Look. I got it. What you got to swap?'

With the time-honoured flick, he laid his swapsies out on the brickwork alongside him. There, glinting in the sun, was the picture of the full Arsenal team resplendent in their red and white shirts. I pointed to it. 'Swap?'

'Ok,' he said, taking the Chelsea card from my hand while I took the Arsenal one from his.

But the trade wasn't over. I had seen that he also had an Arsenal player in his swapsies, one that didn't have. If I could add it to my collection, I'd have a full-house of the Arsenal team card *and* the three players, a complete set of the team I'd supported since my dad had taken me to Highbury two years before. I pointed to the card. 'How about swapping that one?'

Phillip scrutinised my fan of swapsies. 'Nah. You got nothin' there I need.'

It was true. After my time in the gang, my swapsies weren't anything special. 'What about two-for-onesy?'

He shook his head. 'Nah.' He pointed at my cards turning up his nose as if they reeked of dead fish. 'Everybody's got those-uns.'

'Three-for-one then?'

He huffed and puffed. 'Make it four.'

Nobody ever swapped four for one but I was desperate. I nodded.

He took my four best cards and handed over 'Tommy Docherty – Wing Half'.

Although I was happy with my acquisition, I had paid a high price. I had crossed a line. Four cards for one! I'd be a sucker for anyone wanting to hold me to ransom unless I could improve my swapsies. But I had what I had and the prospect of getting better ones was bleak when I could only buy a few at a time and Christopher Allen held so many.

I strolled over to a quiet corner of the playground and looked around before taking my collection out of the inside pocket of my school blazer. I undid the rubber band and carefully inserted the two new cards into their correct places.

After school, still buzzing from the four-for-one trade, I decided to visit the stagnant pond. It was in a copse on the edge of the greenbelt and stank. We carried bricks to it from the nearby bombsite and lobbed them in to make the noxious gases bubble up while the bricks sunk slowly like they were in quicksand. According to our schoolboy mythology, the pond had no bottom.

Under the shelter of the trees I took out my cards – the collection not the swapsies – and slid out the Arsenal ones. I laid them on the sawn top of a tree stump smooth with age. I surveyed the four of them together for the first time: The Arsenal Team, Jack Kelsey – Goalkeeper, Tommy Docherty – Wing Half, and David Herd – Centre Forward. The beam on my face must have lit up that whole wood.

Voices of approaching kids came from the other side of the pond and I ducked down. I was too late. David Rowe had spotted me as soon as he entered the clearing. He pointed. 'Hey, look. It's one of the Eclands. He's on 'is own. Let's scrag 'im!'

The first to move was his fighting lieutenant 'Scatty' Basset who was renowned for flying at his opponents with his arms flailing like a dervish. I didn't fancy a bundle with him so I ran. I ran for my life.

I was fast enough to stay well ahead of the gang but I didn't dare slow down until I was back in the residential streets near home. All I could picture was the Rowe gang gathered around the tree stump, whooping and hollering like savages as they celebrated the capture of my Arsenal set. I imagined them passing the cards triumphantly from grubby hand to grubby hand before David Rowe took it upon himself to flick my treasured collection dismissively into the stagnant pond.

I was bent over, gasping for breath and tears streamed down my cheeks as it all fell into place. This day would be every day from now on. Was it too late? Would Richard Ecland let me back in the gang?

Rooting for Change

Lemn Sissay MBE

So Britain has left Europe? A man leaves a woman. He packs his things and goes. He tries to convince her that she's useless. She mourns the loss but in time she celebrates freedom. Yes it was a shock for her but she starts to reassess the relationship and realizes he was a bully. He was petulant. He was a control freak.

It's a cold winter. He looks back. He has thoughts. The door is closed. He tells himself he didn't want to be there anyway. That's why he left.

Time passes. Not much time passes. He realizes the things he didn't notice at the time are what he's missing. He tells anyone who will listen that he's happy. He goes out to clubs. Alone. He gets drunk and dances. He becomes an island. Nobody wants to dance with him. Screw them he shouts outside the club at 2am. She was a control freak!

Late at night he sends her emails to negotiate how they should communicate in future but she has set his email address to go straight to trash. Meanwhile he tells anyone who will listen how important he was to her. The newsagent watches as he roots for change.

He's afraid. He may not be the man he thought he was. And he is fearful of who he's going to become. It's cold. He's got less money. The roof in his lodgings is leaking. He will tell people that he's having his apartment renovated. But he doesn't own it. His landlord is in Dubai in the sun by a pool.

He hates the landlord. He wants a fight. A serious fight. A fight that will make everyone come onto his side. Everyone will support when they see what a fight he's gonna have. He will have allies again. Allies. He stays in his one room. Plotting.

Finding My Inner European

Ken Smith

1947. The steps of St. Peter's Church Woolwich. My father not long demobbed in a civilian suit, looking very pleased with himself; my mother, petite, pretty, looking confidently at the camera, optimistic about married life in a new country.

This is one of the few photographs I have of my mother in which I can identify the people with her. Almost all the family and friends pictured in the albums she brought with her from her earlier life in Germany, remain anonymous. In the sixteen years I knew her, before her untimely death at 53, she spoke always with great longing for her home, her 'Heimat', and yet she had cut herself off from it. I doubt if I will ever know why she did this but she left me gazing into a space filled by the ghosts of an inexplicably out-of-reach German cultural inheritance, seen through the veil of nostalgia and yearning with which she surrounded it.

My parents met when my father was a member of the British occupying forces in the Ruhrgebiet, a heavily industrialised area of north-western Germany which had been a key target of the Allied bombing. Bochum, my mother's home town, saw a hundred and fifty air-raids after which only 1% of homes were undamaged and 70,000 inhabitants were left homeless. But love blossomed among the ruins, by no means the only instance of an English soldier and a young German woman falling in love. The combination of a brighter future away from the devastation, and my father's strong attachment to his family, meant that it was England where my mother came to settle.

But settle was something she never quite did. Many of my memories of her are centred on the distresses of her homesickness, as she wandered baffled and ill at ease through her life in England. She endured a profound culture shock which persisted until she died. English and German affability had, to her mind, very different rules and, with very few exceptions, she never penetrated beneath an English informality which confused her; one which seemed to signal openness but which in the end always held back from allowing a closer connection. There were undoubtedly other factors in my parent's life together, and my mother's expectations of it, which contributed to her disenchantment; they perhaps created a sense of shame over the life she was living, when she compared it with the memory of the one she had left behind. With her own mother in Germany having died young only a few years after her arrival here, and as an only child, perhaps she felt there was nowhere she could go back to.

I remember that moving our family to Germany was briefly considered during my childhood but this was long before the EU made such transpositions possible. My father's time there had given him a great affection for the country but he would have had to start out again as a Gastarbeiter, a guest worker, not an attractive proposition even from the perspective of the modest but safe conditions in which we were living. With memories still fresh of the urban poverty of those around him in his youth in southeast London, such an adventure would have carried too great a risk; and so the notion evaporated.

My knowledge of Germany was to be as a holiday-maker years

later, with many happy weeks walking in the forests and visiting galleries and historical sites. But never Bochum. I suppose there was a spell around it that I felt I didn't want to break, a spell woven by my mother's recollections of it. Her tales and those photos had created in my mind a place of warm conviviality and a more affluent, sophisticated life; of stylish hats and close friendships; a place deliberately broken from and forever longed-for. For me it held the glamour of the unknown and stood in imagination for one kind of German-ness: green stemmed wine glasses, cake with whipped cream, the importance of rules in helping people live together, a sense of what is right and what is wrong and a readiness to express it, the particular music of the language, town and country close together.

But a couple of years ago, for reasons I still can't quite pin down, I decided finally to visit. Well off the tourist path, Bochum is not really a place that pulls in foreign visitors, in spite of having a significant art collection, a reputable theatre and a never-ending run of Starlight Express. Perhaps because of this, Bochum has kept a calmer, more humane atmosphere than some of the larger and more famously attractive places targeted by tourists. Unlike some other towns and cities in Germany, it has not invested greatly in recreating its pre-war cityscape and has instead installed modern glass and concrete cubes to house its shopping opportunities; though some of the results have a degree of elegance about them, curving along the wide boulevards with a softer modernism.

A few echoes of the old city still whisper through the present one, mostly in the reassembled stones of the churches. On the site of the medieval marketplace, stands a statue of Fritz Kortebusch and his faithful dog , a replica of one that was melted down in the war. He was the last city cowherd, running the residents' cows and goats through the city and out to the pasture where the Stadtpark now is. He did this until 1877, by which time the city's population had grown enormously with the industrialisation of the Ruhrgebiet and Bochum was no longer a small rural town of farmers and craftsmen. The locals still put flowers by the statue. The story is that Fritz used to dine at the nearby Altes Brauhaus Rietkötter, tucked away behind the shops; the oldest surviving secular building in the city. A Gasthaus since the mid-eighteenth century, it's busy on the evening when my wife, Valerie and I visit, all the tables in its typically German wooden interior lightly laden with conversation and Westfällische specialities. It's easy to imagine my mother here, sitting in a corner with a cigarette, a glass of something and a few friends.

I had a couple of her papers, from among those which my father had passed on to me some years ago when I had started researching my family. Included in them was a doctor's letter confirming my mother's fitness to travel to England. This gave me the address at which she had been living and a focus for the visit. A little way out towards the edge of the city, we find it still standing, part of a series of apartment buildings: survivors, restorations and new builds. Together they form a façade of varying colours and textures, not quite blending but certainly not clashing. A gentler note is added by a line of slender trees running along the street. The year of its construction appears high up in moulded plaster, indicating that it is one of the few pre-war survivals. On a quiet morning gazing from the opposite side of the road, it's oddly gratifying to see it in such good repair, the spring sunshine showing it off at its best. I might persuade someone to let me take a look inside one of the apartments but no-one emerges for me to accost. I feel certain anyway that no-one in the family has lived there for a long time.

To give another focus to the visit, I had considered while planning it the possibility of visiting the grave of my grandfather, who had himself died young during my mother's childhood. There are only four entries in the German family record book, 'Familien-stammbuch', that had been among my mother's papers. From this I knew that, though my mother had grown up in Bochum, her father had died in the nearby town of Castrop-Rauxel. I had writ-ten to the town archive there asking if they could tell me precisely where his grave was. A chain of enquiries followed, with my letter forwarded a couple of times, finally reaching the relevant ceme-tery office. Frau Frank, an official there, replied to confirm the place and date of his burial, and also that she had found some of my relatives, who would be in touch shortly. This was wonderfully generous of her and totally unexpected. A few days later Hans, whose grandfather had been the brother of my grandfather, and who lives in Castrop-Rauxel, did indeed get in touch, sending me an e-mail to introduce himself.

To have a branch of the family in England came as a great surprise to Hans. The fragmentations of the war meant that the memory of my mother's existence and her departure for England had been long lost among the family remaining in the Ruhrgebiet. My German grandfather's early death had, I suspect, very likely resulted in my mothers' closer ties being with the numerous aunts in her mother's family. Even though Hans had known one of my mother's cousins, a couple of whose letters were in my mother's papers, he had no idea that as a young man he'd had an aunt living across the North Sea.

Hans and Karin, his wife, come to our hotel in Bochum, sweep us up for coffee, cake and champagne at their home, where we meet his brother Günther and his partner. Refreshed and fully wel-comed, we are taken to the Friedhof Bladenhorst, a forest ceme-tery where the abundant azaleas and the lushness of the spring greenery offer further welcome. Although the memorials have long gone, Hans has tracked down the graves of my grandfather and of our great grandfather; we stand there together, before visiting the graves of his parents. Far from being morbid, visiting the cemetery is a cheerful and fitting way of commemorating our new connection. This, of course, needs consolidating further with dinner, which soon follows in a favourite local restaurant, where we are proudly introduced as cousins from England. We could not have expected a warmer, more open-hearted welcome.

Those couple of letters from my mother's cousin were not only evidence that she wanted to resurrect her connections with her family in Germany, not long before she died; they also offered a clue as to the deeper roots of the family. In one of them it states that her grandfather, Konrad, had been a miner and had originally come from Friedewald in Hessen, some way southeast of Bochum over the border in another land; furthermore, at the time of her writing in 1975, members of the family still lived there. So in parallel to planning the visit to Bochum, I found myself speculatively writing to someone with the family name listed in the on-line German telephone directory.

With my letter I included a very rough family tree, the record of a conversation with my mother over the kitchen table in my early teens; and a photograph of a family group which I thought might be of Konrad with his wife and children. A couple of weeks later, I received an e-mail from Bernd, the son of the now elderly recipient of my letter, in which he told me that we were indeed related; and that Konrad had been the brother of his great-grandfather. I learned later that there had been a short trend in Germany for individuals unexpectedly and fraudulently claiming a family connection in the hope of financial gain. That Bernd also had a photograph of Konrad assured him that my approach was a genuine one. It seemed oddly appropriate that this email arrived on Armistice Day.

The e-mail was soon followed by a phone call from Bernd's daughter Maren, a keen family historian. She had built an extensive family tree tracing the family back to 1642, to which she gave me on-line access. From having very little information about my German antecedents, I had in a couple of months, and with a little serendipity, found two sets of cousins and knew that the family had deep roots in heart of the country. And I, the unexpected English cousin, had the pleasure of introducing them, the unacquainted German cousins, to each other.

Valerie and I visited Friedewald after walking for ten days through the intense greens and blues and blazing sunshine of the Hochr höner, a long-distance trail southeast of there. In contrast to Bochum, Friedewald is a small country town, though again with its own uneven mix of old and new, following the catastrophic fire of 1875 when most of the town accidentally burnt down. There are a few surviving timber-framed houses in typical Fränkisch style and some later reconstructions; otherwise it's mostly modern suburban in appearance. The centrepiece of the town is the Wasserburg, an imposingly solid castle that recalls the town's former significance standing at the crossroads of two important trade routes, when the locals had an imperial licence to charge a fee for providing safe transit through this part of Hessen.

Surrounded by a wide moat, it's a fine ruin now. Beside it lies a broad courtyard, one side of which is devoted to the Heimatmuseum, giving fascinating insights into the social history of the town. In a cabinet on the ground floor, alongside some antique miners' equipment, a couple of certificates catch the eye. They commemorate twenty-five years' membership of an association of miners and were issued in Bochum. The museum attendant tells us that we need not be so astonished at this coincidence, as numerous people left the area to work in the mines of the Ruhrgebiet; so many that they earned the soubriquet of 'Westfalengänger' – 'Wanderers to Westphalia'. The growth of potash mining in Hessen and Thüringen created movement between the Ruhr and the

Rhön, this part of Hessen. In the case of my great-grandfather, it seemed ultimately to be a one-way trip, raising his family in the Ruhrgebiet during the last years of the cowherd's rural labouring. He never returned but he left his photograph behind.

We have a similarly warm greeting from the Friedewald cousins, who take us on a short tour of the town and pointing out its significant features and places with a family connection, shielded by their umbrellas against the torrential rain. There is another cemetery to visit, this time a more modest affair on the edge of the town where lies Georg, the person to whom I had sent my letter but who died before we could meet.

It's unlikely that I will ever be able to identify many of the people in my mother's photo albums. But making these connections with living members of her family, has provided a compensation for the mystery that surrounds those depicted in them and for their being long gone with only the faintest of traces. And in a way it's enabled me to identify myself a little more clearly, giving some solidity to the legacy of my mother's homesickness, a legacy which has left me feeling curiously displaced. So many genealogical quests seem to be connected to place, to require a visit to the locations which feature in the family history – as if being there will somehow provide insights or some obscure resonance with which to deepen an identity, to find a meaning that will fit more warmly than your usual everyday clothes. I can't say that I experienced profound epiphanies on my visits to Bochum and to Friedewald, more just a sense of something at last coming to rest and a deep gratitude for the warm welcome we received.

Some years ago, I visited Sparsholt, the village in Berkshire where my paternal grandfather was born. Though I knew him only later when he lived in London, seeing the villages in the Vale of the White Horse where he and his forebears lived offered a view into another source of identity. I remember him as a kind man, still essentially a countryman, sleeves rolled up, a ginger moustache and an aroma of pipe tobacco; following the form of the horses, scraping out the ashes from the coal fire, enjoying a crusty loaf and piece of strong cheddar. He and the place of his growing up stand for one kind of Englishness, which seems to fade as England changes: a kestrel hovering, a sweep of green hills, butterflies, real beer in ancient pubs, keeping things in proportion, forbearance and fair play.

As I try to make sense of why England is wrenching itself away from Europe, I sit and wonder at the world's short memory. I think of my Berkshire grandfather, gassed in the trenches during the First World War, moving with my grandmother between bomb-damaged homes in London during the Second. I remember seeing my father's photographs of the destruction in the Ruhrgebiet. I've learned during these family history researches that I had great-uncles who were imprisoned in concentration camps, one of them murdered there. And I remember the weeks spent walking in the forests of Germany and over the hills of England. From all this remembering comes a hunger for harmony and more gratitude – for the decades of peace since 1945.

Coming back from Bochum, sitting on the plane as it slowly taxies out to the runway at Düsseldorf, I feel someone touch my shoulder. I turn around to see if it is the person in the seat behind me trying to attract my attention but the headrests form a solid barrier through which no-one could have reached. I look at Valerie beside me but she is quietly reading, hands resting on her book. The engines roar. The plane surges forward and lifts itself into the sky. Perhaps my mother had made it back home after all.

Je Suis Européen

George Szirtes

1

I have the badge that does what badges do.
The badge declares. Behind the declaration
a vast silence. In the silence voices
that inhabit silence as they would a city
complete with landmarks, full of silent statues
that speak the city into ordered being.

What is the city? What is the silence doing?
Whose are the voices wandering among statutes?
Where do the voices lead? Whose are the petty
quarrels embodied in a street map that retraces
its own history and turns it into fiction,
and which of these fictions should we regard as true?

2

Silence is cacophony with the sound turned off.
Cacophony is Bach, Haydn and Mozart carved
into statues with open mouths, surveying
our disasters and turning it into music.

There are reasons for living here. There is
the music, there are statutes in the streets.

There are also the dead in their brief notes,
those missing from archives, stalls and shops that close
and vanish. There is the constant background musak
we all move to in the silence without trying.
There is everything we have made and have deserved.
There is the silence. The sneeze and the dry cough.

3

I am a citizen of an overdressed republic
that knows itself as more than an illusion
and will keep donning clothes and moving on.
Sometimes I think I too am overdressed.
I think I should strip naked, walk the street
with nothing on, and face the filthy weather

we emerge from. I think *I* is another
as we all are. I think it's getting late
and dark. It's hard to see. I smell the dust
that's everywhere and settles. I know it mine.
I am in love. I am standing at the station
waiting to board. I'm not about to panic.

Europe

Stephen Timms MP

I campaigned energetically in my constituency for a Remain vote in the referendum last year. The result was a small majority locally for Remain. But I spoke to many constituents in the campaign who intended to vote to Leave the European Union.

There are wholly honourable reasons why people wanted to leave. In particular, the European Union seems much too impervious to democratic scrutiny. But the problem with leaving is the economic penalty we will have to pay. A hard Brexit would mean thousands of jobs being lost, as swathes of economic activity – from financial services to car manufacturing – would re-locate in order to stay inside the single market. My conclusion is that – like Norway today, a country outside the European Union – we need to stay in the single market.

As a member of the single market but not of the EU, we will be subject to all the same rules, but no longer have any say about what the rules are. After all the turmoil of the referendum campaign, I accept that it would be hard to defend that outcome. But it would be harder still for the government of the day to defend the economic dislocation that would be triggered by leaving the single market.

And perhaps – if we stay in the single market – we can fashion a future for ourselves which is distinctively British, where we do have a say over what the rules should be, and in which those who felt so strongly that Britain should 'take back control' would recognise that there had been progress.

Democratic scrutiny in the EU

Henry Tate opened his Thames Refinery in Silvertown, in my constituency, in 1878. Sugar has been refined there for 140 years, and several hundred people work there for Tate & Lyle Sugars today. When Britain joined the Common Market, it was important for the British government to secure fair competition between sugar produced by the two methods: processing beet grown in Europe, and refining cane imported from developing countries in the Commonwealth. For over 40 years – with ups and downs – a reasonably level playing field was maintained.

But that all changed with the revision to the Common Agriculture Policy which took effect in 2015. All the previous restrictions on beet production were lifted; and all the restrictions on cane imports were left in place. The economics of cane refining in Europe were wrecked.

I have never seen any statement from the Commission to justify this change. In so far as I can understand what happened, it appears that the Agriculture Commissioner – a Romanian – saw an opportunity to give a boost to beet farmers, and grasped it. The well-being of people working in refineries – and of farmers growing sugar cane outside Europe – were of no interest to him.

I asked to meet the Commissioner before he made his decision. He declined to meet me. Instead, I met an amiable official from his office, who told me nothing useful at all. And the Commissioner went on to wreck a significant element in the agreement which allowed Britain to join the Common Market over forty years ago.

How did this happen? In part, it reflected the weakness of David Cameron's government in Brussels. He always sounded sceptical about the EU, and so had little goodwill in Brussels to draw on. One of his first decisions as party leader was to withdraw Conservative members from the main right-of-centre grouping in the European Parliament. There was an immediate loss of British influence over decisions made in Brussels. The British government found it increasingly difficult to get its way. The Romanian Commissioner would not have been able to get his way if Tony Blair and Gordon Brown had still been in charge in London; but David Cameron had never bothered to build the support which they had. British policy failures – and, from a national perspective, the one over sugar was just a small example – contributed to the growing surge in Euroscepticism.

In Britain, if a Minister makes a decision which people are unhappy with, the Minister can be compelled in Parliament to provide a justification. In Brussels, in practice, no such mechanism appears to exist – even if, in theory, the European Parliament should be able to deliver it. The Agriculture Commissioner, if he was even aware of anger that he had wrecked the economics of cane sugar refining, suffered no discomfort as a result of it.

And I understand why so many people in Britain concluded that we don't want our country governed in that way.

Dislocation of a hard Brexit

In the year following the referendum, I paid two visits to the impressive high tech campus of Rolls Royce Deutschland at Dahlewitz, near Schönefeld airport, some forty minutes' drive south of Berlin. 3000 people work there. It has played a key role in eco-

nomic regeneration in the former east German state of Branden-
burg since it was established, as a joint venture with BMW, in 1993
– a pioneering choice so soon after the re-unification of Germany.
It builds and maintains aircraft engines, working very closely with
the Rolls Royce factory at Derby, and now represents about a quar-
ter of Rolls Royce's worldwide activity.

What will be the effect of introducing customs barriers between
Britain and Germany when we leave the EU? Companies like
Rolls Royce have integrated manufacturing across the EU, so parts
and components often cross national boundaries several times on
the way to producing a final product. What will happen if duty has
to be imposed every time an item moves to or from the UK? And
how will potential future customs delays change manufacturers'
decisions about where to locate their European operations? Will
staff be able to move readily between their employers' plants in
different countries? At Dahlewitz, I met several British staff worried about their future.

German leaders at Rolls Royce Deutschland told the delegation
I was in that – for German high tech companies – British universities are the best research partners of any in Europe. But, once we
leave the EU, and no longer participate in Europe-wide research
projects, working with British universities may well no longer be
practical.

Japanese car manufacturers have enjoyed enormous success
with their plants in Britain. The Nissan plant in Sunderland is
the most productive car factory in Europe. UK plants have to
fight against competition from other sites in Europe every time
the companies' leaders in Tokyo are planning a new investment.
The odds will be hugely stacked against them if products made
in Britain – mostly for export to Europe – have an import duty
imposed on them whenever they cross the Channel.

The prospects for UK financial services, denied the advantages of barrier-free access to the European single market, look bleak too. Already, major initiatives have been launched from Paris, Frankfurt and Dublin to attract banks and insurers from London, and decisions to re-locate have already been made. One respected estimate is that 70,000 financial services jobs will go.

Ministers understand these dangers. They claim that their negotiations in Brussels will secure 'barrier-free access' to the European single market, while we no longer comply with the rules – especially over free movement of people, and decisions of the European Court of Justice – which have been difficult for the UK in the past.

The problem is that the outcome Ministers promise is not, in fact deliverable. As one German civil servant put it to me, *'if you want the benefits of the single market, you have to obey the rules of the single market.'* In discussions with dozens of German parliamentarians since the referendum, I have yet to meet a single one who would be willing to vote for the 'have your cake and eat it' outcome which UK ministers claim they will deliver.

The Germans are very polite about it. They express admiration for Britain, and for Britain's contribution to and influence in the EU. They explain how dismayed they are that Britain is planning to leave. They say that Germany will be Britain's best ally in Europe after Brexit. But it is to them self-evident that no country can 'cherry-pick' the parts of the single market arrangements which suits it. If Britain was permitted to do that, then other countries would pick the bits that they wanted too – and in no time the European single market would collapse. That is a risk no German parliamentarian is prepared to contemplate.

One compromise suggested to me in Germany was that we should re-define free movement. We should say that we would be prepared for European citizens with firm job offers in the UK to come freely, but not otherwise. It would be 'free movement of labour', in line with the original aspirations of the Treaty of Rome, rather than the free movement of people which it has evolved to. It was suggested that, if Britain was willing to do that, then we could secure largely barrier-free access to the single market.

But I fear the window for securing that outcome – if there ever was one – has now closed. It would have required the British government to focus all its negotiating firepower on achieving it. Instead, it has said it isn't interested in any kind of free movement, and even suggested that people in the EU should be subject to the same immigration rules as people from the rest of the world. A compromise along these lines is surely now off the table.

Stay in the Single Market

So my conclusion is that, for economic reasons, we should stay in the European single market and the customs union.

Some argue that we can replace our current markets in Europe with new markets in faster growing, more dynamic areas of the world economy. In time, that might be possible – although it might not. But to leave the European single market in March 2019 would create immediate economic dislocation, and disrupt the means to earn a living for thousands. No government should contemplate imposing such hardship on so many of its citizens, even if was utterly convinced that better times would follow a few years down the line.

The most immediate problem with staying in the single market and the customs union, while no longer belonging to the EU, is that we will continue to be bound by all the rules but no longer have any say over them. It will be difficult to justify such an outcome after all the turmoil of the referendum, the change of Prime Minister, and the subsequent general election. People will ask whether so modest a change in our circumstances really warranted all the upheaval.

But if we leave the single market, and find ourselves suffering the burden of import duties, unfamiliar customs bureaucracy, price rises, restrictions on our movements – and a significant degree of unemployment – then the politicians responsible for that will have a far harder time of explaining themselves. And those will be the consequences.

I have heard repeated assurances from Brexit supporters in the Commons that the EU will grant us barrier-free access to the single market, because they export so much more to us than we do to them. This is a fallacy, as anyone who has spent any time discussing these matters with parliamentarians in Germany quickly learns. It is estimated that 60,000 German jobs depend on car exports to the UK. It's a large number – but smaller than the number of jobs created in Germany last year. And there is no way that Germany will sign up to an agreement which, for them, would put at risk the continuation of the whole European project – which has made such an enormous contribution to German prosperity and peace – simply to maintain 60,000 jobs in the car industry.

The only way forward now which avoids severe economic damage – other than deciding to stay in the European Union after all – is to stay in the single market and customs union. If we do that, we will have to find ways to influence the rules – which will continue to apply to us – and we will need to work for arrangements which we can live with – for example over free movement. And, I would argue, the sugar market. But at least, along that road, we will have a chance.

Taking the other road, the government would never be forgiven for contriving an economic dislocation blighting the lives of tens of thousands.

Inside the Bubble

Heather Welford

It happened in March 2016, three months before the referendum:

I was on a train due to leave London Kings Cross at about eight pm... except there was some delay further up the track which meant we were stuck there, with the prospect of a slow, slow journey up north once we did get going. Brits normally compelled to sit and eat and breathe close to each other, possibly for hours, in silence, started to sigh, exchange frowns and tut loudly.

As the train finally started to move, the trolley distributed free soft drinks and sandwiches, by way of apology. Some passengers took out biscuits and choc bars, and began swapping battle stories of previous delays. The thirty-ish guy next to me opened a bottle of rosé wine, asked the trolley server for paper cups, and offered it with a flourish round the four people at our table and the two across the aisle. Ooh, thanks!

We were all white, none of us had a foreign accent, and this, I think, led Wine Guy to feel emboldened.

'Now we're all talking,' he said, 'I just want to say one word to you all to get your reaction...'

We looked at him, a bit warily.

'Brexit!' he said.

I think we might have returned to our iPads and newspapers, but he was on a roll.

'Go on,' he said. 'What do we all think?'

He had a shiny, enthusiastic face, and I pegged him as some sort of salesman. Once you have accepted a slug of someone's supermarket rosé, you probably feel less able to wriggle out of an actual conversation – whether it's about widgets and sprockets, or referendums.

He asked each of us, and the replies included, 'I'm not sure I know enough about it', 'I'm still thinking, to be honest', and 'I have to register to vote first – not sure if I'm eligible' from a young man while a woman who said she was a law student said, 'I think probably 'leave'... to which Wine Guy actually punched the air and said 'Wahey!' so I now knew for certain which side he was on.

My turn.

'I live in France a lot of the time,' I said, 'so that's an influence on me... I'm going to vote 'remain'...'

I might have said more, but his face had twisted.

'France?' he said, or rather spluttered. 'Ugh... France! How can you live in France?' He shook his head in despair. 'I hate France, me.' He had a sort of grin on his face, probably conscious he'd gone a bit far, and thought the smile might soften the words, and make them sound teasing, even bantering.

I was at a loss. The other passengers said nothing. They were waiting for my reaction. I mean... how do you defend an entire country in that context? Should you try?

He went on. 'It's the French who are behind the whole EU thing anyway,' he said.

'Please don't say "straight bananas",' I thought to myself.

'I mean, straight bananas, and all that,' said Wine Guy.

'That's a myth,' I said.

'Well, it might be,' he agreed, 'but it's the principle, isn't it? We have to take back control, we have to be in charge, we shouldn't have the French telling us what to do!'

I tried to make a few points about the elected European parliament, about co-operation and mutual respect, but shortly afterwards I replaced my large, noise-excluding headphones, declined a biscuit and opened my book. I was aware the talk went on without me – but I had no other exchanges with Wine Guy until he got off at Durham and grinned a farewell. 'Good luck to you – enjoy France!'

The incident was my first direct experience with someone whose whole attitude to Europe was the opposite of mine – that 'referendum bubble' where people who think one way rarely meet people who think the other way was real, and the reason why so many of us woke up the morning of 24 June utterly poleaxed (including David Cameron).

Since then, I've added the episode to the discussions on radio phone-ins, and the vox pops on TV, and the online posts I have read. I am on one side of what we now know is a poisonous divide in UK public life, that shows no signs of closing. Wine Guy's outlook continues to echo – we 'have to be in charge'.

I'm on the side where people don't 'hate' other countries' nationals, or view them with automatic suspicion; I regard with scepticism or outright disbelief stories about Christmas being banned in Birmingham and Easter eggs being rebranded in Tesco's; or tales of recently-arrived Eastern Europeans being awarded a palatial council house plus £KKK of handouts each month.

I'm on the side that feels acutely uncomfortable at the way some people – the ones outside my bubble – have found validation for their irrational dislikes. I understand resentment at being 'forgotten' or 'unlistened to', and the feelings of powerlessness – but I despair at how these resentments have focused on immigration issues.

I don't think there has ever been good evidence, pre- or post-referendum, to show that leaving the EU will bring prosperity and fairness where it's needed; it's even acknowledged by die-hard Leavers that some people may be worse off than before. I don't think any of the economic forecasting had much effect on voters' choices, or their support, one way or the other, then or now.

Instead, too many Leave voters have either been overt in their xenophobia, or have used the notions of sovereignty and 'control of our borders' as a fig leaf for their real motivations. This is not full-blooded racism – though of course it can be. Hate crimes involving religious and racial attacks and discrimination rose 23 per cent in the year after the referendum, according to a Freedom of Information survey carried out by the Independent. But more often, it's a populist nostalgia that persists in some daft idea that Britain is best and we don't need anyone else – which is echoed, as we now see, all over the world – and indeed, that membership of the EU threatens us.

The EU is in a strong position to tackle the three huge issues of the twenty first century – namely climate change, global migration, inequality. These can only ever be dealt with together, and certainly not in economic isolation. The UK should be part of peaceful, co-operative progress towards a resolution of these planet-sized problems.

I'm still massively disappointed the Remain campaign didn't reflect any of this. It relied on stalwart volunteers like my ex-Labour councillor friend who dutifully manned street stalls and leafleted, but who complained bitterly that support from the leadership was barely visible. 'Most people I speak to don't even know Labour is supporting Remain,' she told me.

The Labour party were reluctant to confront their traditional voters – largely Leavers – with any sort of passionate argument in favour of staying in. This was, and is, partly a fear of sounding like a middle class elite scolding the working class for their old-fashioned views, and partly to do with the Old Left's belief that the EU is a continent-wide Boss's club.

Events since then have shown the Labour party hunkering down in order to preserve party unity, with opposition to 'hard Brexit' turning out to be the best we can hope for at present.

I sometimes imagine Wine Guy and his ilk seething with frustration that we're still 'in'. The knotty problems of our unpaid but legally binding EU bills, the challenges of the border between Northern Ireland and the Republic, let alone the status of semi-detached ex-pats like me, are irritating barriers against 'control'.

They just want to be out, highly suspicious that support for any sort of negotiated, nuanced 'soft Brexit' is a potential enabler – a way to allow for a return to the EU, some day.

I really hope it is.

Afterword

The idea for the anthology started as a challenge to myself: I wanted to be persuaded that leaving the EU was the right decision. The vague optimism and speculation of the pro-Brexit negotiators didn't inspire much confidence. In my opinion, and as David Lammy MP said, the 2016 referendum was advisory rather than legally binding and I was puzzled why some political party leaders were so eager to invoke Article 50. And as Armando Ianucci suggested, a cross-party group of MPs should have led the negotiations.

The anthology is about Europe, not just the EU, but in the interests of fairness we tried to include more pieces in favour of Brexit. Alas, it proved difficult to be more even-handed. (In addition to the issue of balance, as we go to press some comments will already be out of date.)

Obviously not all aspects of Brexit, such as agricultural subsidies, the impact on the environment, the wishes of Scotland and the thorny matter of Northern Irish borders, have been scrutinised here.

But as William Keegan said:

'So what hope is there, other than "events" – which may not be welcome in themselves, but which might provoke a rethink about this colossal waste of time and resources being devoted to Brexit? (I should much rather be writing about something else, by the way, but I regard this as the biggest crisis of my journalistic career.)'

When the referendum was announced, my main reasons for voting to remain in the EU were that it would be too arduous and too costly to negotiate our exit speedily. Imagine having to deal with 27 partners rather than one as in any normal divorce settlement. Being in the EU, regardless of its many faults, is safer and the lesser of two evils, especially when world leaders in other continents are behaving in unpredictable ways. And, it is better to reform an institution from within rather than abandoning it altogether in what seems like an isolationist, obstinate and tax-avoiding frenzy.

There might possibly be eventual benefits in leaving the EU, but it could take a generation. Whatever happens, the poor and disabled will still be disaffected. As Giles Frazer pointed out, the protest vote to leave the EU was a way to publicise the underprivileged plight and if we do suffer another economic crisis, at least the advantaged will know what it feels like to be disadvantaged.

The true tragedy is that Brexit is a distraction from far more important problems needing to be addressed such as: the refugee crisis; climate change; financial and banking reforms; scrutiny of offshore tax havens and money-laundering; not forgetting what's happening in the White House. This isn't the time to sever our close ties with the EU.

Patricia Borlenghi

Acknowledgements

We are very pleased this project was met with such enthusiasm.

Firstly, thank you to our contributors and to the editors, Anna Johnson and Anna Vaught. Thanks also for the help of Mark Brayley, Sue Jacquemier, Nicky Hamlyn and Charlie Johnson.

Attila the Stockbroker – thank you for your poem!

DNA by Christine De Luca is published with kind permission from *Dat Trickster Sun* (Mariscat Press 2014) and the Italian edition with kind permission of Nuova Trauben Publishing House published in *Questo sole furfante*, Torino 2014, translated into Italian by F.R. Paci.

Professor Michael Dougan – thank you for your article!

Canon Giles Frazer – this article was originally published in The Guardian on 11 February 2016 and is reproduced by kind permission of the author.

Andrea Inglese – his poem in the original French is also published in France.

Baroness Helena Kennedy QC – part of this was published in The Guardian on 3 May 2017. Baroness Kennedy kindly gave permission to publish her whole article.

Lemn Sissay MBE – thank you for your text!

About the Contributors

Anna Johnson *www.ajbooksandbags.com*

Suzy Adderley *www.suzyadderley.co.uk*

Maurizio Ascari *https://www.unibo.it/sitoweb/maurizio.ascari*

Attila the Stockbroker *www.attilathestockbroker.com*

Wersha Bharadwa *wersha.co.uk*

Mark Brayley *https://markbrayley.com*

James Coiley *is a financial services lawyer.*

Catherine Coldstream *www.catherinecoldstream.com*

Christine De Luca *www.christinedeluca.co.uk*

Uwe Derksen *http://uwederksen.com/me*

Professor Michael Dougan *www.liverpool.ac.uk/law/staff/ michael-dougan*

Canon Giles Fraser *www.theguardian.com/profile/gilesfraser*

Rick Garboil *trained as a scientist and enjoys playing the piano.*

Cecilia Hall *is an artist and printmaker.*

Andrea Inglese *www.nazioneindiana.com*

Helena Kennedy QC *www.helenakennedy.co.uk*

Professor Jean McHale *is Director of the Centre for Health Law, Science and Policy at Birmingham Law School.*

Petra McQueen *www.thewriterscompany.co.uk*

Giacinto Palmieri *youcancallmegiac@gmail.com*

Robert Ronsson *www.robertronsson.co.uk*

Lemn Sissay MBE *www.lemnsissay.com*

Ken Smith *www.kensmithcoaching.co.uk*

George Szirtes *georgeszirtes.blogspot.com*

Rt Hon Stephen Timms *is Labour Member of Parliament for East Ham.*

Heather Welford *www.heatherwelford.co.uk*

Further Reading

Darren Anderson https://www.prospectmagazine.co.uk/magazine/how-the-irish-border-could-derail-brexit

Roxana Barbulescu and Jean Grugel https://www.academia.edu/23493423/Unaccompanied_minors_migration_control_and_human_rights_at_the_EUs_Southern_border_The_role_and_limits_of_civil_society_activism

Julian Barnes https://www.lrb.co.uk/v39/n08/julian-barnes/diary

Tony Connelly https://www.rte.ie/news/analysis-and-comment/2017/1117/920981-long-read-brexit/

Jonathan Cooper http://www.doughtystreet.co.uk/documents/uploaded-documents/David_Camerons_Three_Big_Mistakes,_written_by_Jonathan_Cooper.pdf

Giles Frazer https://www.theguardian.com/commentisfree/belief/2017/oct/12/still-puzzled-by-the-brexit-vote-take-yourself-off-to-blakenall-heath

Jens Geier https://www.theguardian.com/commentisfree/2017/oct/18/thersa-may-brexit-eu-european-parliament

A C Grayling http://www.theneweuropean.co.uk/top-stories/a-c-grayling-has-6-reasons-to-prove-why-brexit-will-be-stopped-1-5098052

William Keegan https://www.theguardian.com/business/2017/apr/09/brexit-hasnt-happened-yet-changing-all-the-time-conservatives

Paul Krugman http://www.independent.co.uk/news/business/brexit-paul-krugman-zero-chance-britain-better-off-eu-leave-single-market-custom-union-exports-trade-a7965871.html

David Lammy MP http://www.theneweuropean.co.uk/top-stories/labour-mp-david-lammy-i-feel-like-an-outcast-in-my-own-party-1-4846982

Jolyon Maugham QC http://www.prospectmagazine.co.uk/magazine/brexit-take-back-control

James Meek https://www.lrb.co.uk/blog/2017/06/09/james-meek/destination-brexit/

Anand Menon http://www.independent.co.uk/voices/article-50-triggered-theresa-may-brexit-brexiteers-europe-donald-tusk-what-will-happen-resign-a7653711.html

Professor Patrick Minford https://static1.squarespace.com/static/58a0b77fe58c624794f29287/t/58a57d943e00be70faaeaf97/1487240621083/UK-WTO-Trade-Strategy-Non-Cooperative-Continent-17-02-2017.pdf

Violeta Moreno-Lax https://www.academia.edu/t/a-LRVavD4-uTsX9/34547322/Accessing_Asylum_in_Europe_Extraterritorial_Border_Controls_and_Refugee_Rights_Under_EU_Law_Oxford_University_Press_2017_

Fintan O'Toole http://www.nybooks.com/articles/2017/09/28/brexits-irish-question/

Beth Oppenheim https://www.prospectmagazine.co.uk/politics/what-explains-the-brexodus-from-dexeu

Andrew Rawnsley https://www.theguardian.com/commentisfree/2018/jan/14/how-and-why-britain-might-be-asked-to-vote-again-on-brexit

Dennis Skinner https://www.morningstaronline.co.uk/a-e4af-Beast-of-Bolsover-Im-voting-out#.WX4JWLDTWhA

Bob and Roberta Smith https://www.theguardian.com/commentisfree/
2017/may/12/brexit-british-art-artists-museums-galleries

Martyn Stanley http://martynstanley.com/ https://www.goodreads.com/
author/show/6545672.Martyn_Stanley

Enrico Tortolano and Ragesh Khakhri http://morningstaron-
line.co.uk/a-6d16-What-we-need-is-a-peoples-Brexit#.WWC77LHT-
WhA

Yanis Vourafakis https://www.theguardian.com/politics/2017/may/03/
the-six-brexit-traps-that-will-defeat-theresa-may?CMP=fb_gu

Refugees and Peacekeepers – A Patrician Press Anthology edited by
Anna Johnson, Patrician Press, 2017